"ope."

One look and her body froze. Right there in the eating sun, she couldn't even feel her heartbeat.

oel Kidd, the boyfriend who'd walked out on her ighteen months ago, stood next to the helicopter.

Black T-shirt, olive cargo pants and sunglasses to ide those dark eyes. From this distance she could ee the ever-present dark scruff around his chin. His black hair was longer, grown out from the short ilitary style she remembered.

he could see the gun strapped to his hip and knew oel knew how to use it. That used to scare her a ttle. Now it comforted her frazzled nerves.

What are you doing here?" The whip of her voice irrored her frustration.

He hesitated, as if weighing what to say and whether o let his question go. Whatever he saw in her xpression had him closing the distance between hem. "I came to find you."

LAWLESS

—

HelenKay Dimon

HARLEQUIN® INTRIGUE®

To my husband for agreeing to watch all those big budget Hollywood action movies with me and pretending I was telling the truth when I called them writing research

Recycling programs for this product may not exist in your area.

ISBN-13: 978-0-373-69760-1

LAWLESS

Copyright © 2014 by HelenKay Dimon

Printed in U.S.A.

www.Harlequin.com

ABOUT THE AUTHOR

Award-winning author HelenKay Dimon spent twelve years in the most unromantic career ever—divorce lawyer. After dedicating all that effort to helping people terminate relationships, she is thrilled to deal in happy endings and write romance novels for a living. Now her days are filled with gardening, writing, reading and spending time with her family in and around San Diego. HelenKay loves hearing from readers, so stop by her website, www.helenkaydimon.com, and say hello.

Books by HelenKay Dimon

HARLEQUIN INTRIGUE
1196—UNDER THE GUN*
1214—NIGHT MOVES
1254—GUNS AND THE GIRL NEXT DOOR*
1260—GUNNING FOR TROUBLE*
1297—LOCKED AND LOADED*
1303—THE BIG GUNS*
1352—WHEN SHE WASN'T LOOKING
1369—COPY THAT
1387—SWITCHED
1434—FEARLESS**
1440—RUTHLESS**
1488—RELENTLESS**
1493—LAWLESS**

*Mystery Men
**Corcoran Team

CAST OF CHARACTERS

Joel Kidd—The former DIA agent endured a rough upbringing with a survivalist father. Joel turned to a life in intelligence work and landed a coveted position with the Corcoran Team, but he walked away from the one woman who meant everything to him. When he gets word she needs help, he comes running. Question is if he'll have the strength to leave her again.

Hope Algier—Hope knows about roughing it. She loves being in the sunshine and thrives on a challenge. She's conquered climbing and archery, and now she's leading outdoor adventures for business executives in need of a little team building. One of the men in her group goes missing in the middle of the West Virginia backcountry, but nothing prepares her for the arrival of Joel—the man she loves but wants to hate.

Tony Prather—The sharp businessman takes struggling companies and turns them around. This time he plans to make a home and be not only the savior of Baxter Industries but its new CEO. First he has to explain some missing money and odd sales figures. Maybe sending his executive staff on a retreat will make the trouble go away.

Mark Callah—Baxter's vice president of finance has a bit of an ego problem. When he goes missing on the business retreat after waving a gun around, no one suspects Hope, but they do wonder if he's a victim or the one firing the shots in the forest.

Jeff Acheson—The blowhard businessman thinks he knows everything. He's also hiding a company secret under all that ego. But when the bullets start flying, which side will he take?

Lance Ringer—He is the lowest ranking executive on the retreat. He also appears to be rock-solid. He's a new dad and the one who stays calm when everything goes wrong. Then again, looks can be deceiving....

Charlie Bardon—As the owner and chef at the camp where the business retreat is being held, he's right in the center of it all. He tries to get the businessmen to safety. He has weapons and skills. He can be a great asset to Hope and Joel...but can they trust him?

Connor Bowen—The leader of the Corcoran Team is wrestling with some heavy-duty secrets of his own, but when his men need him, he appears. He's focused and determined, but everyone wants to know the same thing—where is his wife?

Chapter One

Hope Algier preferred sunshine and fresh air to a stuffy office. Except today.

She spent most of her life outdoors. Her father had tried for years to entice his baby girl into the boardroom of the family business with promises of expensive cars and impressive bonus packages. She turned them all down without a second thought, but right now a leather chair behind a big desk sounded good.

Trees towered over her and surrounded her on every side. This section of land adjacent to West Virginia's Cranberry Wilderness was called the Cranberry Backcountry for a reason. It consisted of more than eleven thousand acres of hills and woods and little else.

Animals skittered around her. Leaves rustled as the summer wind blew warm air under her ponytail and across the back of her neck. Thick branches blocked most of the sunlight, giving her an eerie sense of isolation.

No people, no houses and no easy way out.

Turned out, this patch of forest messed with her satellite phone. She needed open sky for a signal, and she could only see peeks of blue through the canopy of summer green leaves above her. Right about now she'd give anything for a second of heat on her face.

She slipped behind a large trunk and leaned against it.

Her heartbeat hammered in her ears as she slipped the sat phone out of the pocket of her cargo shorts. It measured a bit longer than a cell phone and fit in her palm. The map she'd memorized earlier and carried in her back pocket pointed to a clearing up ahead. She hoped she was close enough to catch a signal.

Please let it work this time.

She pushed buttons. When that didn't do anything, she smacked the side, hoping to jolt it into action. She even thought about smashing it against the cushion of dirt and leaves under her hiking boots.

She was about to repeat the hitting cycle when something crunched off to her right...again. The same subtle crackling she'd been hearing on and off since she'd dove deep into the trees. A squirrel, probably. She repeated the comment in her head over and over, hoping to reassure her brain and stop the sudden subtle shake moving through her hands. She refused to think bear or, worse, predator of the two-legged kind.

As she shifted, the stray branches scratched her bare legs and caught on the short sleeve of her cotton tee. She balanced her head against the hard bark again and counted to five. It took all of her control not to call out for Mark Callah, the vice president of finance for Baxter Industries.

He'd been all gung ho about "roughing it" on this corporate retreat. So much so he had brought a gun along without telling her. She saw it when he had waved it around last night at dinner. As the person leading the retreat, she had confiscated it. That didn't go over well. Now he was missing.

Crack.

There it was again. That made the fourth time she picked up the sound she wanted to write off as nothing.

Something furry and four-legged and small…she hoped. But the gentle thuds sped up.

She peeked around the tree she was using as a shield and spied what looked like a flash of blue in the distance. The same flash she'd seen twice so far on this journey to find Mark and grab a clear shot to the satellite to jump-start the phone.

She'd left the rest of the executives back at camp with orders to make breakfast and clean up. Except for Mark, they weren't exactly the venture-out-alone types. She strained to remember any of them wearing navy this morning at roll call, but her brain refused to focus.

Crunching and snapping echoed all around her until she couldn't tell from which direction the noises origi-nated. The tunnel effect had her doubting her hearing and her vision. If she spun around one more time or ventured too far in any direction, she'd need the GPS to guide her back to camp.

What she really wanted was a view of open sky. If she could get to the edge of the field and send out a call for help, then she could duck back into the woods again.

Maybe she could lure out her visitor. Not that the op-tion sounded too reassuring to her right now.

Without thinking, she reached for the leather sheath hooked to her belt. Her fingers skimmed over the hilt of her knife. She wanted to slide it out for protection, but running on uneven ground with a blade struck her as a distinctly stupid thing to do.

Still, having the makeshift weapon lessened the anxi-ety pounding through her. A little.

With one last glance into the thick columns of trees be-hind her, she took off. Her hands swatted at the branches blocking her forged path as her feet slipped over rocks and roots and her pace picked up to a jog. The wind whistled by her and the slap of leaves hit her face. She made enough noise to put a target on her back, but she didn't care. She needed that open field.

Footsteps fell hard off to her left this time. The thump of shoes against the ground kicked up and the person drew almost parallel to her position. She tried to zigzag even though she knew her white shirt would give her position away…wherever she was.

But she needed space and enough distance to make the call and pull her knife. Regardless of whatever or whoever else was out there, she would not go down without a fight.

The trail in front of her brightened and sunlight puddled on the forest floor. Even without the thinning of branches she knew she was close from the beep of her GPS as she zoned in on the preset location. The sat phone smacked against her leg with each step. She fumbled to pull it out of her pocket and hold it as she ran.

The log came out of nowhere. A fallen tree too thick to jump over right in her path. She tried to pivot and her ankle turned. One second she was on her feet and the next her knee cracked against the hard ground and something sharp dug into her palm.

She was down for only a few seconds but long enough for heavy breathing to pound in her lungs and float through the trees. The labored sound drowned out everything. The running near her seemed to stop. She feared that meant someone or something circled nearby ready to grab her.

Ignoring the pain thumping from her foot to her hip, she pushed up. With her hands on the log, she skirted the end and ran. Each punch of her right foot against the hard ground made her teeth rattle with the need to cry out.

But the bright light was right there. A few more feet

and she'd be free. She dodged a massive tree trunk as the crashing of footsteps beside her picked up again. A blue blur raced close enough for her to make out a figure, but the heavy hoodie pulled down low made it impossible to identify who it was.

But the *who* didn't matter right now.

She broke into the clearing and reached into her pocket for the phone. Nothing. She patted her shorts and spun around in a circle as desperation swamped her. Fear rumbled through her until her knees buckled.

The log. The fall. The memory came rushing back. She must have dropped the stupid thing on the ground when she went down.

With her back against a tree, she scanned the forty feet of open field in front of her and the miles of woods beyond that. She tried to calm her breathing and slow her heart enough for her to concentrate.

The adrenaline kept pumping. She knew she should welcome it because it kept the pain at bay and her mind off the blood around her knee and throbbing in her hand, but she needed to focus.

The figure, whoever it was, stood still, right behind a tree about fifty feet away. She slipped her knife out again and tightened her grip over the handle, ignoring the fresh burst of throbbing from her injury. She opened her mouth to call out, to make the idiot face her instead of trying to terrify her in silence.

A strange thwapping drowned out her yell. She shielded her eyes with a hand and squinted up into the sun. Blue skies greeted her. She didn't see anything, but the noise grew louder.

Whop, whop, whop.

A helicopter broke into sight as it came in for a landing. She blinked twice, not trusting what she was seeing. Out here, in the middle of nowhere, it didn't make sense.

Her breath hiccupped as a new panic crashed over her. She could have walked into anything. Drug runners or criminals of any type. And if the pilot was a partner to her tracker, there was no way a knife would save her.

The helicopter hovered over the ground. The blades kicked up grass and leaves. When it finally touched down, she could make out two men, but the glass, and probably the waves of fear, distorted her view.

She was about to slip back into the blanket of the woods where she at least stood a chance when the rustling off to her left had her attention dragging back to the tree and the person hiding there. The hoodie was gone. Fearing the attacker could sneak up on her, she backed to the edge of the open field and held her knife in front of her as she faced the woods.

"Hope."

She thought she heard her name over the chopping of the helicopter blades, but she knew that wasn't possible. No way had one of her executives ventured away from the camp and somehow made it this far.

Her mind had gone into shutdown mode. That was the only explanation. She was hearing things and jumping at every sound.

The helicopter's engine wound down and the propeller slowed to a lazy turn. The change had her spinning around to face the new threat. One look and her body froze. Right there in the beating sun, every organ inside her whirred to a stop. She couldn't even feel her heartbeat.

"Hope, what are you doing?" Joel Kidd, the boyfriend who had walked out on her eighteen months ago rather than fight for a life with her, stood next to the helicopter.

Black tee, olive cargo pants, and sunglasses to hide those near-black eyes. From this distance she could see the ever-present dark scruff around his chin. His black hair was longer, grown out from the short military style she remembered. He might even have been thinner. And none of that explained what he was doing in West Virginia.

With one last look into the menacing woods behind her, she stepped forward. She could see the gun strapped to his hip and knew Joel was well trained in how to use it. That used to scare her a little. Now it comforted her frazzled nerves.

"You cut your leg." He ripped his sunglasses off, and concerned eyes traveled over her. "What's going on?"

Seeing him hit her like a kick to the stomach. She almost doubled over from the force of it. She'd loved him and mourned his leaving, then had spent some time pretending she hated him. As she looked at him now, old feelings of longing came rushing back. So did the urge to punch him.

"What are you doing here?" The whip of her voice mirrored her frustration.

He hesitated as if weighing what to say and whether to let the question go. Whatever he saw on her face or in her expression had him closing the distance between them. "I came to find you."

"Why?" Truth was, he devoted his life to gathering intelligence and protecting others. Right now she could use a bit of both.

The sound of the helicopter seemed to have scared off her tracker, and for that reason alone she was willing to hear Joel out. For a few seconds.

"You haven't been picking up your phone." His gaze

did another bounce up and down her body, hesitating over her torn-up knee. "Where is it?"

Good question. "Lost."

His near-black eyes narrowed. "Really?"

"Long story."

"Any chance of hearing it right now?"

"First, you answer a question of mine." She glanced past Joel to the pilot. He jumped down and headed for them.

"Shoot," Joel said.

"There is no way you just happened to be out here, tooling around West Virginia, when you live in Annapolis. So, what's going on?"

The corner of his mouth lifted in a smile. "You know where I live now?"

No way was she walking into that discussion. "Let's stick to my question."

"Fine, it's not a coincidence." Joel's expression went blank. "Your father sent me."

Figured. "It's still your turn to explain, so keep talking."

She loved her dad, but his protective streak stayed locked in hyperdrive. He ran a private security company, one Joel used to work for. All that danger made her dad a bit paranoid. Though, admittedly, in this instance that was a good thing.

"Your dad and Baxter Industries." Joel shifted his weight, putting his feet hip-distance apart. "Seems your dad wanted you to have backup out here. Combine that with the twitchiness of the Baxter Board about having a twenty-six-year-old woman, alone, guiding the male executives, and you get me."

"How very sexist of them."

"They clearly don't appreciate how competent you are outdoors."

She had no idea if that was a shot or a compliment, so she ignored it. "If the phone isn't working, how did you… oh, right. The GPS locator still functions."

"Yes."

"So, Dad tracked me down and sent you by helicopter."

Instead of answering, Joel motioned to the pilot. "This is Cameron Roth."

She wasn't in the mood for meeting people just now, but there was no reason to be rude. "Okay."

"We work together," Joel explained.

"At where exactly?" She'd tried to find out where Joel went when he left her dad's company. One night, bored and feeling lonely, she conducted a search, hoping to locate him, and uncovered nothing.

Her father finally let slip Joel lived in Annapolis, less than an hour away from her place in Virginia, the same place he used to live with her but never bothered to visit now. Being ignored made her stop checking in on the guy. If Joel didn't care enough to make contact, she wouldn't either.

"Ma'am." The other man butted in with a nod of welcome. "You can call me Roth or Cam."

The guy looked about the same age as Joel, a few years older than her, and shared Joel's used-to-be-in-the-military look. Broad shoulders with muscles peeking out from under the edge of his T-shirt. They both carried their bodies in a permanent battle stance, as if they could shoot or tackle at any moment, if needed.

Joel had the Tall, Dark and Whoa-He's-Hot thing down. That hadn't changed in their months apart. Cam's lighter hair and blue eyes made him seem less intense, but knowing the male type standing in front of her, she doubted that was actually the case.

Joel clapped. "There. That's settled."

Looked like the menfolk thought explanation time was over. She disagreed. "Let's go back to my question. Why are you really here? And skip the sat phone talk this time."

"Your father sent me to look for you." That smile widened. "Now it's my turn to ask a question."

"Did you really answer mine?"

Cam laughed. "She has you there, man."

Joel nodded in the direction of her hand. "Is there a reason you're carrying a knife, or is the plan to stab the helicopter?"

She glanced down, then back at Joel. "Are you worried it's meant for you?"

"I take it you two know each other pretty well," Cam said.

The conversation kept jumping around. She'd only remembered the knife when Joel mentioned it. The burning from where it pressed into her palm suddenly hit her.

Then Cam's comment grabbed her attention.

"Joel didn't tell you who I was to him?" She wanted not to care, but the hurt swallowed up her indifference.

Cam looked from her to Joel and back again. "Let's just say I'm thinking he left out some important pieces about your joint past."

"Hope." Joel snapped his fingers and brought the focus back to him. "The knife?"

She stared at it in her hands. "What about it?"

"Why are you holding it as if you're ready to attack?"

She couldn't come up with a reason to stall and certainly had no reason to lie. Not about this. Not to him. "Someone was following me."

Both men leaned in closer, all amusement gone from their faces. Cam's mouth opened, but Joel was the one who barked out a question. "What?"

Now that she had their attention, she decided to spill it all. "And I think one of my executives might be dead."

Chapter Two

Joel called up every ounce of his practiced control to stay calm. Before he'd joined the Corcoran Team, a private security organization out of Annapolis, Maryland, that specialized in risk assessments for companies and governments, this sort of thing would have had him spinning and drilling her with questions.

Connor Bowen and the rest of the Corcoran Team had taught him the importance of patience and holding still for the right opening. Without those skills, the high-priority, under-the-radar kidnap and rescue missions they conducted would fail. Because when you worked outside the legal parameters and without a safety net, mistakes couldn't happen.

After a lifetime of kicking around in the intelligence field, Joel knew he'd finally landed in a place that felt right. He'd buckled down, used his tech skills to fill in after the last tech guy left and tried to forget about her. Hope, his greatest weakness.

Now he seriously considered telling Cam to get lost for a few minutes, though he doubted the guy would budge. Not when he was staring as if he'd never seen a woman before and was hanging on every word of the discussion.

Joel couldn't really blame Cam on the gawking part. Hope looked as good as Joel remembered. Better, even.

The long dark brown hair and near black eyes hadn't changed. From the dimple and girl-next-door hotness to the tanned legs and smokin' petite frame, he found her almost impossible to resist.

Add in her smarts, competency with weapons and near fearless determination when she wanted something and he'd had no choice but to dump his job and move to the next state to keep from falling deeper into her. Or that's what he'd rationalized at the time.

But right now he worried more about the danger that appeared to be haunting her. "Say that again."

She cleared her throat. "I have a missing executive."

Joel had no idea what that meant. "You said dead a second ago."

She shrugged. "I'm hoping that was an exaggeration."

Well, that cleared up…nothing. He glanced over at Cam.

He shook his head. "Got me. I have no clue."

"Hope." Joel reached out to touch the hand with the weapon in it and felt the subtle tremor running through her. Yeah, forget how comfortable she looked hanging around outside, something bad had happened and she was throwing off the desperation vibe.

His protective instincts kicked into high gear. He folded his hand over hers and slid the knife out of her palm. Not an easy task since she had a death grip on it.

Moving nice and slow, he eased the blade back into its case at her waist as he rubbed his thumb over the deep creases on her palm. "Where is this executive?"

"His name is Mark Callah."

"Okay." Joel didn't dig too deep for details. Not yet. "Where is Mark?"

"I have no idea since I lost him."

Cam grunted. "She's giving you a pretty logical answer, actually."

"I got up this morning and he was gone from camp." She tugged free of Joel's hold and rubbed her hands together. "I headed for this clearing to use the sat phone and realized some guy was following me. Then your helicopter—"

"Hold up." For the second time, she jumped right past the most interesting part. "Go back a second."

"To where?"

Stray branches crunched under Cam's feet as he shifted his weight. "I'm guessing to the 'following me' part."

She spent a second frowning at both of them. "Blue hoodie. The guy stalked me, then started moving faster and came up the side until we were parallel. He didn't look up and stayed close. Your helicopter scared him off."

"Stalked?" Joel didn't hear much after that word.

"Yes, Joel." She didn't roll her eyes, but she looked like she was right on the edge of doing so.

She could sigh at him all she wanted because he was not letting this conversation drop. Not until he assessed the level of danger. "Could this person be one of the executives you have out here on the team-building retreat?"

This time her face went blank. "Wow, my dad really did fill you in on this job."

"Let's stick to your story for now." One more diversion and Joel worried he'd never be able to pull the tale out of her. And he knew from experience any talk about her dad and his protective nature would not make this exercise go faster.

"Except for Mark, most of the Baxter Industries management talk tough but are terrified of being out here. One guy jumped around demanding to go home because he found a tick on his upper arm." She snorted. "I mean, come on."

Joel bit back a laugh. "Very manly."

"Right. So, you understand why I can't imagine any of them chasing me through the woods, being covert and ducking out of sight for no good reason."

"You're throwing out some scary words there."

"So?"

She could shoot and run and build a camp from twigs, but that didn't make her invincible. He wondered if she understood that. "My point is this story gets worse the more details you add."

She glanced over her shoulder and deep into the woods behind her. "Anyway, I'd like to think if it was one of my guys, he would have helped or at least called out when I fell."

The bad news just kept coming. Joel glanced at Cam. "And now we have a fall."

She faced them again. "What?"

"You skipped that part before," Cam said.

Joel guessed that was intentional. "Let's just say your linear storytelling needs work."

"I'll run through all of it if you need me to—"

"I do." Joel wanted her comment to stop right there.

She talked right over his interruption. "But since you're here, you can come with me while I get my sat phone and then we can spread out and hunt for Mark."

Joel caught her in the second before she took off. Never mind her tale about a stalker and the terror in her eyes only a few minutes ago. Now she was ready to head out. "I thought you lost the phone."

"Yeah, but I know where."

"Your definition of lost is no better than your story-telling ability."

"We don't have time for chitchat." Her gaze dipped to where his fingers wrapped around her elbow, then bounced back up again. "I'm assuming you guys need to get out of here and head off to some other covert action-movie adventure, so let's move."

Nice try. "You're my job this week, remember?"

"Yeah, we're going to talk about that later."

"Talk all you want. I'm staying." That had been the plan before the knife and the story about the fall and every other bizarre fact she threw out, and he wasn't changing it now.

But there was some good news here. Her feistiness clicked back into place with full force. While the verbal jabs about his job used to drive him nuts, he missed this side of her, too.

She didn't back down. She didn't care about his size or ability with a weapon. She understood he'd never hurt her and held her ground. Probably had something to do with having a former special ops father who made sure his precious daughter and only child could protect herself no matter what.

The attitude had gotten her in trouble more than once. Not with him, but some of the men in her father's business, Algier Security, didn't appreciate her refusal to be a good little girl and sit down.

Sexist idiots.

Still, she could be rough on the male ego. He glanced over at Cam to fill him in with a simple explanation. "She doesn't approve of what we do."

"Understood," Cam said with a nod.

Hope wasn't having any of it. She shot them both one of her men-can-be-clueless frowns. "That's not true."

Cam kept nodding, as if he'd figured out some great big secret. "Is that why you left him?"

Damn. "Let's not go there." This was just about the last topic Joel wanted to discuss.

Strike that. It was *the* last. Dead last.

"I figured it out." Cam smiled. "She's the ex."

Suddenly Joel regretted that one night a month or so ago with too much beer and too much talking. Cam had wanted to know why Joel never dated and he mentioned a tough break-up. Cam clearly put it all together.

"Didn't he tell you the story?" Hope's eyebrow lifted. "Interesting."

"How so?" Cam asked.

"Joel left me."

Cam's eyes bugged as his jaw dropped. "No way."

"I know, right?" She shook her head. "Whatever."

Cam whistled. "I didn't see that news coming."

That was enough of that. Joel cleared his throat to get everyone's attention. "Can we get back to the missing guy and the stalking?"

"Camp is back here." She didn't wait for a discussion or arguments. She headed off through the thick branches, with twigs and other debris crunching under her boots. She slowed down only long enough to glance over her shoulder and gesture for them to follow.

"Hope…and she's gone." Joel took a step in the same direction.

Cam slid in and blocked his path. "You dumped her?"

"Let it go."

Cam laughed. "I think we both know that's not going to happen."

It was a long story and Joel knew he didn't exactly come off well. With his messed-up upbringing, a quiet life in the suburbs wasn't on the table. But she had tempted him, made him think even for a little while that he could do normal. Then he got offered a dream job with the Defense Intelligence Agency and, like an idiot, picked it over her.

Funny how karma nailed him on that one.

Cam leaned in with a hand behind his ear. "Not talking?"

"Nope."

"You will." He winked, then called out to Hope. "Hey, where was this stalker walking?"

She stopped and gestured to the line of trees directly across from her. "About fifty feet that way, running parallel with me."

Joel tracked her white shirt as she pushed long branches out of her way and kept walking. "Notice how she acts like whatever happened wasn't a big deal."

"Was she ever an operative?"

"Mountain climber, archery expert, like Olympic skill level, outdoors type and can shoot better than some members of the Corcoran Team."

"You're talking about Ben, right?" Cam asked.

Ben Tanner was the newest member of the Corcoran Team and a former special agent for NCIS. The guy could shoot but he lacked the sniper skills of many on the team. And they never let him forget it. "Obviously."

Cam stopped staring at Hope, and it looked like that took some control on his part. "Explain to me why you left her again? Because, gotta be honest, man, between the way she looks, the way she moves and that list of skills you just read off, I think I'm in love."

"Get over it."

Cam nodded, which he often did. "Ah, okay. Interesting."

Hope's white shirt got farther away. That meant one thing—the time for talk had ended. "Stop with that crap."

Just as Joel lost sight of her, she peeked out from behind a massive tree trunk. "You guys coming?"

This time Cam laughed. "Your ex wants your attention."

"Don't call her that." Correct or not, the term grated on Joel's nerves. It meant she was free to find someone else, and even though he knew that was fair and the right thing, he despised the idea.

He'd spent the months away from her pretending he didn't care when her father had called to alert him that she'd gone out on a date with this guy or that one. The old man was on a warped matchmaking mission. One that slowly broke Joel until he thought he'd go insane imagining her in bed with someone else.

"I am so happy I was available to fly you in for this op. Wouldn't have missed this for anything." Cam clapped Joel on the back. "Not sure who will enjoy this more—the guys back at the Annapolis office or the guys on my traveling team. Tough call."

Both options sucked for Joel. "I could hide your body out here."

"You're welcome to try."

Because Cam came to Corcoran with the nickname "Lethal" and rumor was he'd flown Navy missions so secret just mentioning the operation names would bring the FBI running with guns firing, Joel decided to switch the subject. "And this is a favor for an old friend, not an op."

"If a businessman is missing and someone is chasing your woman, it's an op." Cam didn't wait around for an argument. He headed in the direction Hope indicated as the stalker's path. "I'll be over there, straining to hear every word."

Joel took off after Hope. She'd stopped, and with his

long stride, he caught up fast. When he drew close he
saw her standing near a fallen tree, staring at the dirt.

"What's going on?" he asked.

She looked up, the anger obvious in her tight jaw and
the flush of red on her cheeks. "My phone is gone."

"I thought we already knew that."

"No, I mean I had it in my hand while I was running—"

"You ran through this?"

"—and stumbled here. I dropped the phone and now
it's gone."

There was no trail and no obvious signs of a path.
Roots poked out of the ground, and the trees had grown
to the point where they blanketed the area. Any sane
person would watch her step. But she had run. Figured.

He thought about lecturing her but abandoned the idea
when she bent down and started patting the rough ter-
rain with her palm. Hope knew the outdoors, loved and
cherished the openness. It was one of the things they
had in common.

Still, a phone could only bounce so far. "Any chance
you lost it somewhere else?"

"No." She tried to reach her arm under the log. "I'm
not exactly easy to spook. I know what I'm talking about."

"But you are."

She tugged on her arm but didn't remove it or sit back
up again. Twisting around, she looked up at him. "What?"

"Spooked." And stuck. He wondered how long it
would be before she admitted that. "Your pulse is racing and you're jumpy. Not that long ago you were shaking and holding that knife like you were ready to slash
anyone in your path."

"Someone was chasing me." She kept shifting and
squirming. The heels of her boots dug into the dirt as
she wrenched her shoulder.

Much more of this and she'd really injure herself. Any second now she'd ask for help. Well, most people would. With Hope, who knew?

He was ready to jump in. She just had to say the word, but he'd bet all the cash on him she wouldn't.

"I get the chasing part," he said.

She stopped moving around and shot him a big-eyed stare. "You don't believe me."

With Hope, he figured that was as close as he was going to get to a plea for help. He crouched and did the quick math on the best angle to pull her out without dislocating her shoulder. "I didn't say that."

"I am not a little girl who needs protecting. Your days of holding that job are over and, in case you missed it, I was never a little girl on your watch."

"Oh, I noticed." He jammed his fingers into the hard ground as dirt and peat moss slid under his nails. Ignoring the closeness and the way her arm brushed across his chest, he wedged his hand under hers and dug a shallow tunnel with his knuckles. "For the record, I noticed everything about you. Still do."

Before he could add to the comment, footsteps echoed around him and boots appeared in front of his face. He strained to look up and got as far as the familiar utility pants.

"Our company is back," Joel said into the relative quiet of the forest.

She tried to spin around and hissed when her trapped arm stopped her movements. It took another beat for her to get a word out. "Where?"

"He means me." Cam dropped down to the balls of his feet with his body between Joel and Hope. "What are you two doing?"

With his hand caked with dirt, Joel wrapped his fingers around her bare arm and gave a quick pull. "Rescuing her."

"I don't need rescuing." She popped free and fell back on her butt. Next she rubbed her shoulder joint. "Ouch."

Joel refused to feel guilty for getting her unstuck when she'd been too stubborn to ask for his assistance. "Good thing you weren't caught then."

"Glad we cleared that up." Cam stood. "She's right about being followed. There are footprints over there."

"Any clue about who or why?" Joel got to his feet and put a hand down, surprised when she took it to jump up next to him.

"Some interesting information." Cam turned his camera around and flashed an image most people would think showed nothing but leaves but really showed an outline of a shoe. "Men's size eleven. Probably a hundred-seventy pounds."

She leaned in closer to the screen, her eyes narrowing. "You can tell that from a grainy picture?"

Cam nodded. "And your stalker is an overpronator."

Joel had to smile at that. "Now you're just showing off."

Cam shrugged. "I'm good at my job."

"Which is what again?" she asked.

No way was Joel entertaining an impromptu debriefing in the middle of an isolated forest. Protocol was very clear. The Corcoran Team operated on a need-to-know basis.

To the world they provided risk assessments and moved in to help if things went wrong. Important but not the complete story. The definition missed the reality of the constant danger and huge amount of shooting.

Fact was, telling the woman he once dated about his

current occupation had to violate some rule. "Not up for discussion."

She sighed. "I've been hearing that my whole life."

A stark silence followed her words. Joel didn't bother to explain the real-world need for not filling her in. She knew how this game was played. She'd lived with a man known for having secrets. Joel got that she hated the game, but that didn't change it one bit.

Cam finally broke the quiet with a clap that thundered through the trees. "So, we have someone skulking around the woods."

"And a missing phone." She turned on Joel with a finger in his face. "Do not ask me if I'm sure this is where I dropped it."

Those words died in his throat because saying them could get him punched. "No, ma'am."

She treated him to a smile then. "That's new."

He tried not to notice how it lit up her face. "I'm not always difficult."

"Yes, you are," she said.

Cam nodded at the same time. "Not always, but mostly."

"We should head back and make sure none of these weekend warriors cut off a toe." Falling back into command mode kept Joel from telling both of them off. "We also need to check out Hope's knee."

She glanced down.

Cam nodded. "Maybe this Mark guy wandered into camp and there's some reasonable explanation for all of this."

The men started to walk but she stayed still. "What about your helicopter and wherever you were planning to go after stopping in here?"

Sounded like she still wasn't understanding his assignment here. Joel tried again. "This is my final destination. With you."

Cam slid his foot over the piles of leaves stacked around them. "And I'm good to hang out for a few hours."

Her hands went to her hips, and her legs still didn't move. "You both think something is seriously wrong."

Joel decided not to sugarcoat this. Sure, the past half hour could mean nothing. Or it could mean Baxter Industries and her dad were right to send in reinforcements. They wouldn't know until they got back to camp. "Stolen phone and a stalker? Yeah, Hope. Something is not right."

Her smile came roaring back. "Good."

He wondered if he would ever understand her mood swings. "How is that good?"

"Because you believe me. You're not writing this off as some hysterical woman thing."

Of all the things she could have said, that one came out of nowhere. "I've never known you to be hysterical."

She eyed him up. "You know, you seem slightly smarter about women now. Maybe some things have changed about you since we last went out."

And he worried the most obvious—how much he wanted her—hadn't.

Chapter Three

Hope tried to ignore Joel for the entire walk back to camp. His constant stream of questions didn't make that easy. He wanted to know about the campers and what her plan had been to get the men in and out of camp. She gave the details, even though she really wanted to stop and demand an explanation for why it was so easy for him to walk out of her life.

Then again, maybe she didn't want to know. Her ego could only take so much, and he had the power to break her. Had from the minute she'd met him.

The forest floor crunched and crackled under their feet. Their steps echoed around her, and Cam whistled as he walked a half step behind her. It all seemed so normal...except for the missing businessman and lost phone. And who could forget the scary stalker?

Amazing how a nice morning could make a left turn into awful so quickly.

She had taken this job to emotionally recuperate. The double whammy of losing Joel and the disaster on her last climbing expedition had sent her world into a tailspin. A new career conducting business retreats and leading simple hiking and camping outings was supposed to be soothing. The way her nerves jumped around was anything but.

"Looks like we're here."

The sound of Cam's voice over her shoulder made her jump and knock into Joel next to her. When her hands brushed against his, a new sensation spun through her. Something like excitement, and that didn't make her happy at all. She wanted to be totally over him, or at the very least not feel anything. She'd do anything for a bit of indifference at the moment.

She settled for doubling her pace and broke through the trees and into the camp clearing a step before her self-appointed bodyguards. The businessmen sat on logs turned into benches around the fire pit area. They looked up as she approached.

They all started talking a second later. Shouting over each other in an attempt to hold the metaphorical floor.

Yeah, she hadn't missed this part of their company dynamic during the past hour.

"Where have you been?" Jeff Acheson, the Baxter director of marketing, dumped his plate on the ground and stood up. His distaste for her was on full display, from his puffing red cheeks to the scowl marring what she guessed most women found to be his perfectly chiseled model face.

She took a long look at him in the bright sunshine and decided he was a bit too buffed and polished for her taste. He had a phony air about him. Probably because he listed his age as thirty-four on the questionnaire she had handed out last night to assess their skill levels, when she knew from the files Baxter gave her the number was more like forty.

That sort of thing struck her as ridiculous. She'd bet he took twice as long to get ready for a big date than she did.

She could still remember the up-and-down sweep he gave her when they'd first met in the Baxter offices. He'd turned on the charming smile back when he thought she was some sort of assistant to the *real* leader on the trip. That disappeared when she'd made it clear she was in charge.

But he picked the wrong time to get all uppity with her. She wasn't in the mood. "Is Mark here?"

"What?" Lance Ringer, the Baxter personnel manager, asked.

Lance was the one guy Hope had liked immediately. He was the youngest on the retreat but didn't try to impress her. He owned up to the fact he hadn't been camping since he was a kid, more than twenty years ago, and would rather be home with his newborn and wife than out roughing it with the guys. Hope found his honesty refreshing.

"Mark was missing this morning and I went to look for him," she said, waiting for Joel and Cam to pipe up and feeling a bit dazed when neither rushed to take the lead. "Did he ever come back?"

Jeff took a threatening step in her direction. "Why didn't you tell us there was a problem before now?"

"Probably because of this type of overblown reaction." Joel morphed from calm to a shield of muscles in two seconds. He reached around Hope, blocking some of her view of Jeff, and put a hand on his chest. "Back up."

Jeff tried to push Joel's hand away. "Who are you?"

"Not relevant at the moment."

Joel didn't move and Cam just smiled. Hope was smart enough to know those reactions meant brewing trouble. Joel's protective nature made it tough for him to back down, and when he was faced with a pontificating blowhard like Jeff, there was no telling what could happen.

"You have a gun," Jeff said.

Joel motioned toward Cam. "We both do."

With the tension building and washing over all of them, she decided this might be a good time to make one point clear. "Joel is my assistant."

She put her hand over his and it dropped away from Jeff. But the battle stance stayed, as did Joel's unwavering gaze on Jeff.

Cam covered his smile with his hand as he mumbled, "This should be good."

"What are you talking about?" Jeff asked as he turned his attention back to her. "I thought you were the supposed leader of this outing."

She said the word *assistant* and Jeff assumed she was no longer in charge. The man heard what he wanted to hear.

Before anyone said anything else that made her grumbly, Hope made the necessary introductions to keep the chain of command clear. "This is Joel Kidd, my helper, and Cameron Roth."

Joel cleared his throat. "Helper?"

With a raise of the chin she held her ground. "Yes."

The silence lasted for only a second before he nodded. "Alrighty then."

Relief poured through her when he didn't push it. She turned back to Lance. "Where's Perry?"

"Who's that?" Cam asked.

Lance got up and brushed off his pants. He stopped to shake hands with everyone. "Perry Kramer is our sales manager."

"What does he sell?" Joel stared at Hope when she shoved an elbow into his stomach. "What? It's a fair question."

Lance shrugged. "But it's probably not important information right now."

Hope heard the rustle of branches and glanced over in

time to see Charlie Bardon, the camp owner and cook, break through the trees on the far side of the last cabin. He was out of breath and running his hands over his grimy chef's apron as he walked.

"What's going on out here?" he asked.

Joel looked to the newcomer. "That was going to be my question."

Charlie didn't look any more willing to back down than Joel. They stood face to face and shared the same former military in-command presence. Pushing fifty, Charlie had been out for decades, but Joel seemed just as determined and set in his ways at thirty-three.

Before this could blow into a full-blown argument, Hope tried to step in. "Mark is missing."

"I was hoping he was with you." Charlie turned his attention to Joel. "Where did you come from?"

Joel shrugged. "Annapolis…or are you looking for an explanation about how birthing works?"

The older man's eyes narrowed. "Are you trying to be funny?"

"Not really."

"Okay, enough." She wasn't sure who deserved the bigger kick to the shin—Joel for acting disinterested and maintaining his monotone voice through the snide comments or Cam, who couldn't stop smiling. "Cam and Joel came in by helicopter to help me."

If possible, Charlie's scowl deepened. "With what?"

She had no idea how to answer the question, so she skipped it and talked to the campers, trying to ignore the fact another one appeared to be missing. "When is the last time anyone saw Mark?"

Taking a long time and making the movement last longer than necessary, Jeff folded his arms in front of him. "When you two fought last night."

Joel turned to face her. "Really?"

"He stormed out, saying he was going to the cabin," Lance said. "But he wasn't in there when I went to bed."

"What time was that?" Cam asked.

"Around midnight."

Charlie blew out a long breath as he talked. "You didn't think that was odd?"

"He was ticked off that Hope took his gun. I thought I heard him coming in later, but he wasn't there this morning." Lance looked at Joel as if he expected backup.

Joel leaned in closer instead. "His what?"

She knew there was no way that comment would slide by. "Gun, and I'll explain later."

"Yeah, you will," Joel said.

But not now. Not when all those eyes focused solely on her. "Go on, Lance."

"That's it. I figured he was walking it off or getting something to eat. Honestly, I didn't think it was a big deal. He got scolded. Get over it."

Hope didn't know what to do with any of that information. Mark had gotten angry and stormed off. She knew that before she took off on her search. But maybe she could get an answer to one question. "Were either of you out in the woods this morning?"

She got a lot of head shaking and mumbling but no answers. She scanned the crowd. Only Lance didn't possess the right body type. He'd joked about gaining more weight than his wife during the pregnancy. Hope doubted that was true, but he was carrying around a few extra pounds that would have made it a bit tough to dodge in and out of the trees.

Still, that didn't mean none of them had done it. Someone had and the nerves jumping around inside her wouldn't quiet down until she had answers, the right number of campers and her phone.

"And where were you this morning?" Joel asked the man in front of him.

Charlie didn't move. "Checking on the food situation."

From the question Hope guessed Joel wasn't as willing to believe as easily as she was. Then again, he'd just met the group, and they were down two members.

"Let's try it this way." Joel shifted his weight. Not a big move. Barely perceptible but something about it made him appear taller and less willing to play games. "When did you last see Mark?"

Charlie's gaze bounced from Joel to Cam and back again. "What's with the weapons? Are you police?"

The look on Joel's face, the way the corner of his mouth inched up, came close to a smile. "Pretend I am."

Charlie didn't share his amusement. "I don't think I will."

Much more of this and they'd never get to an answer. As it was, Lance and Jeff stared, watching the verbal volleys with their mouths hanging more open with each sentence.

Hope decided to act like what she was—in charge. "Charlie, help me out here. Mark wandered off and now I don't know where Perry is."

"I'm pretty sure Perry is in taking a second run at the chow line."

This time the relief walloped the air right out of her lungs. "So, you've seen him this morning?"

Charlie nodded. "About fifteen minutes ago."

"That's a relief," Lance said.

She saw Joel opening his mouth to say something and jumped in first. "But it doesn't explain the Mark issue."

Charlie waved her off. Even threw in a "bah" right before he started talking. "He's just blowing off steam."

The men kept saying it, but the explanation wasn't good enough. "I can't find him and I need him to check in before we do one more thing."

Jeff swiped his thermos off the ground. "We need to go out looking for him."

"How exactly?" Joel asked.

The question caused Jeff to go still. "What?"

Hope knew where this was going. She felt the conversation rolling downhill and couldn't grab a two-second break to throw her body in front of it.

She couldn't speak for Cam's expertise, but she guessed it was off the charts. But Joel knew everything about surviving outdoors. He was the one person in the group better at outdoor activities than she was, and that was saying something.

He thrived in this environment. His father had groomed his kids to fight and shoot, readying them for the domestic civil war he insisted was coming.

Lost in paranoia and reeling from the unexpected loss of his wife, Joel's dad believed the government had lost its way and only small pockets of freedom-loving people would save the world. He went about it by toughening up his kids, making them sleep outside and denying them an education until the state stepped in.

The upbringing was sick and wrong and it shaped Joel in ways she still hadn't explored. He liked to joke and act as if certain things didn't bother him, but she knew. But there were times when his gaze would wander and those dark eyes would glaze. He'd go to whatever place he built in his mind to find normalcy. And he wouldn't let her in.

"Do you know anything about wilderness survival?"

His voice stayed deceptively soft as he aimed the question at Jeff.

The other man held eye contact for a few seconds, then broke it. "We studied up before we came out here."

"Oh, good." Joel stared at Cam. "They studied."

She got the point, but the conversation promised to run them right into a brick wall. "Joel, that's enough."

Not that he heard her. He continued to stare at Jeff.

She knew the hard truth. None of the testosterone-jousting did anything to help them locate Mark.

"Which cabin belongs to this guy?" Cam asked.

"That one." She pointed to the building directly next to where hers sat in the middle of the makeshift line. Because she appreciated the assist, she followed Cam's lead. "Charlie, can you take the guys and put together some provisions? If we're going to spread out and search for Mark—"

Joel frowned. "Are we?"

"—they need to be ready."

Charlie started shaking his head before she finished the sentence. "I'm not convinced this is necessary. He's probably sulking. Struck me as the type."

"He's the vice president of finance," Jeff said, as if that explained everything.

When Joel finally performed that eye roll it looked like he'd been dying to do since Jeff stood up, it was obvious he wasn't convinced. "So?"

But she had a plan and it depended on everyone agreeing and moving on. "Charlie, if you could, maybe, keep everyone together, that would be a great help."

He stared at her, not saying a thing. A gust of wind shook the leaves and the sun beat down on the campground, but the silence stretched out. Finally, Charlie began a slow nod. It picked up in speed as it went and seemed to last for a long time. "Ah, got it."

She blew out the breath she'd been holding. It scratched her throat as it rushed out. "Thanks."

"Gentlemen?" Charlie motioned for the managers to follow him. "Let's go find Perry and get packed."

Joel didn't speak until the place cleared out and the voices faded as everyone slipped through the path between the cabins and headed for the kitchen cabin and open seating area about thirty feet away before he faced her. "What's with the search party talk?"

"Some of this crew think they are mountain men. I was worried they'd run off with butter knives and try to slay bears or something equally stupid." She'd dealt with the type for a long time and developed some skills, the top one being not to let them rally and slide into attack mode.

Cam nodded. "You wanted Charlie to keep them occupied while we searched."

She looked at Joel, waited for him to say something. She expected a lecture on knowing the parameters of her job and leaving the investigation to him, the professional.

Instead a smile broke across his lips. "Your dad would be proud of your covert abilities."

The compliment rushed right to her head, making her as dizzy as drinking the finest wine. "You don't grow up with a former special ops guy and not learn a few things."

That smile only widened. "Apparently."

"Besides, Charlie gets it. He knows the kind of people who come out here," she said, hoping to focus on all she had to do and drag her mind away from Joel. "He can help."

Cam chuckled. "If Joel doesn't tick him off."

Very true. "Well, there's that."

They walked to Mark's cabin. The men's footsteps matched and she had to push her gait to keep up. They had long legs and moved quickly and quietly. She had a case of nerves that shook her hard enough to knock her over. She wanted to believe there was a reasonable explanation, but as the minutes passed her faith waned.

She used her master key to open the lock. All three of them stepped inside and stopped. Their shoulders touched and they still took up most of the open space.

They kept silent as their gazes scanned from wall to wall. The room consisted of two double beds and a small sitting area. With only a few suitcases, a coffeepot on a hot plate and rows of clothes on hangers inside the open closet, the visual inventory didn't take long. There was one door, which went to a bathroom only slightly larger than a closet because the shower was outside the cabin in every building but hers.

Joel's shoes scraped against the wood floor as he stepped farther inside. "There's not much here."

She had to take the blame for that one. "I found I have to really limit what they can bring along or some folks come out here with laptops and three suitcases and think someone else will drag it along."

"Very practical." Joel rummaged through a duffel bag on the floor and peeked under the cushions on the loveseat.

Metal screeched as she slid the hangers on the old rod. She spotted a few shirts and extra sneakers on the floor. There wasn't as much as a chest of drawers in the place.

"Blood." Cam didn't add anything else. One word and so deathly serious.

She spun around to find Cam standing by the bed closest to the door. "What?"

Joel got there first, but she was right behind. They all crowded around the bed, staring and unmoving. No one touched anything.

She tried not to state the obvious, but she didn't see anything except crumpled white sheets and a stack of pillows with a clear head indent in them. "What am I looking at?"

Cam nodded in the direction of the bottom of the bed. "The underside of the cover."

Before she could reach over, Joel put out an arm and held her back. Two steps put him at the small table on the other side of the room. He was back in a flash with a pen in his hand.

With the tip, he lifted off the cover and flipped it back. Dark streaks ran about a foot along the underside. Splotches stained the navy blue blanket underneath. The dark shade hid the color. But she knew.

The dizziness hit her full force and the room spun. She would have grabbed for Joel but he'd crouched down to study the bed close up.

"It's not a lot," she said, looking for any positive spin on this horrible find.

"Well, it's more than a few drops," Joel said. "Almost like the spill of a glass of something."

"Are you sure it's blood?" She wanted them to say no, but she knew they wouldn't.

Joel stood back up. "Not without tests, but I think we should assume it is until we see Mark walking around here."

"Maybe he cut himself and didn't tell me?" She was willing to believe anything at this point, so long as the man was healthy and fine.

"What about this gun?" Joel asked.

The question shot out of nowhere and slammed into her with the force of a body blow. They could add the weapon to the list of things suddenly gone missing.

Dread washed over her and she would have sat down hard on the floor, but Joel reached over and settled a hand on her elbow. Technically, he wasn't holding her up, but inside she felt as if he were holding her together.

She tried to explain over the knot of anxiety wedged in her throat. "Unbeknownst to me, he brought it along. He waved it around at dinner, acting like a big shot."

"Guy sounds like a jerk," Cam said.

She felt obligated to defend him on some level. "He was showing off, but my rules are clear. No weapons."

Joel shrugged. "I'm armed."

"So am I," Cam agreed.

They acted as if they were the only ones concerned with safety. "Yeah, well, that makes three of us."

Cam smiled. "Really?"

"We all know the most dangerous person in a situation like this is the nervous novice with the gun." Joel nodded and she took that as approval and kept going. "I can't have people out here with weapons, or sooner or later one of them will shoot off a hand by accident."

He looked around the room. Even opened the bathroom door. "So where is it?"

"What?"

"The gun."

"I have it." She remembered the fight and what she did. "It's in a small lockbox in my cabin." But somehow deep down, she knew it was gone.

Joel stopped in the middle of the room and fixed her with a serious glare. "A hundred bucks says it's missing."

Just went to show how alike they were. She knew, he knew. Heck, maybe even Cam knew.

Still, she had to ask. "Why would you say that?"

Joel didn't hesitate. "Experience."

Chapter Four

Ten minutes later Hope had her leg wound bandaged and cleaned by Joel and carefully kneeled on the floor of her cabin, putting as little weight on the injury as possible. After a quick check under the bed she sat back on her heels and stared up at Joel. "Can I panic now?"

As far as he was concerned, they'd passed that point one missing businessman ago. "Soon."

Joel had come out here as a favor. He'd dragged Cam because he needed a ride. Now they had a full-fledged mess on their hands.

Time was the issue. Mark had been missing for potentially twelve hours or more. That amounted to an emergency. The weather had stayed warm, but the breeze had kicked up and the air carried the scent of rain.

From all accounts Mark wasn't a seasoned hiker. Animals, accidents, falls—the list of dangers went on and on. He could be hurt or worse.

Joel needed to get word to the rest of his team in Annapolis of the potential issue in West Virginia. They might need search and rescue, or air support, and he sure as hell wanted an answer to who was stalking Hope.

Then there was the bigger problem. The lingering sense of something being off. This should have been a routine assignment for Hope. He understood her dad's worries, and Joel shared them when it came to her safety around a bunch of idiot men in the middle of nowhere, but this felt bigger. Targeted.

Joel didn't like it, and the frown on Cam's face and way he walked around, staring at the floor, suggested he wasn't a fan either. Joel wanted to chalk it up to the mix of guilt and want that pummeled him every time he looked at Hope. She was the one woman who tempted him to give it all up and hunt for a normal ending to his story.

Leaving her was the one time when he'd acted like a complete jerk with a woman and deserved a swift kick. He was lucky she hadn't treated him to one.

But the tic in the back of his neck wasn't about his feelings for her. He loved her until he couldn't see straight. Probably always would. No, this was something else.

He'd been attuned to danger—real danger, not the kind his father manufactured in his sick head—since he joined the military to escape his childhood. He learned to recognize it during his short tenure at Algier Security and honed it at the Defense Intelligence Agency. With Connor's help and the support of the Corcoran Team, he understood not to ignore it and instead figured out how best to handle it.

And he was into it up to his eyeballs now.

"Let's do a weapons check." Joel touched a hand against the gun strapped to his side, then performed a mental rundown of the rest. One at his ankle and the two knives hidden under his clothing, plus the others in the lockbox on the helicopter.

He glanced at Hope. "What do you have?"

"Charlie has a gun." She stood up next to Joel at the side of the bed. "I have a knife and a bow."

"Bow?" Cam broke off from his staring to watch her from across the mattress. "Is that really practical?"

That was the kind of talk that usually led to a demonstration. People underestimated Hope. They saw the pretty face and tight body and decided she must be the type to sit on daddy's piles of money and do nothing.

Joel had made that miscalculation for exactly three minutes before he saw her do a verbal takedown of a guy in her father's office who called her sweetie. Joel had been about to give the guy a lesson in respect, but she'd handled it.

And he'd been hooked ever since. He found other women attractive, but none of them were her. None came close.

He decided to fill Cam in on the nonprivate part. "She was basically a Junior Olympics champion."

"Not just basically." Bending over, she pulled the case out from under the bed and opened it. "Want to see my medals? I have several bows—recurve, long bow and a few compound. You'll have to trust me that I know how to use all of them."

Cam stretched and looked over the bed from his side. "Why did you bring one here? That one's recurve, right?"

She flashed him a smile. "The man knows his hardware."

"Definitely."

"Well, I figured I could show the men how to use it. People generally assume it's easy and have no idea how much strength it takes. And…" Her smile grew to high wattage as she closed the case. "Having a bow and arrows in the room tends to cut down on drunken male idiocy."

That time Cam laughed. "Impressive."

"What do you guys have?" she asked as she sat on the bed.

The laughter in her voice caught Joel in a spell. Seeing

her lighthearted and happy, if only for a few seconds, touched off something inside him.

Near the end they had fought a lot. Then he'd made her cry. He could have gone a lifetime without seeing that, without having her despair rip through him, shredding him from the inside out.

He forced his attention back to the present before the old feelings of guilt swamped him. "Guns, knives." Joel thought about a man tracking her through the woods. "My bare hands."

Her head fell to the side and her hair cascaded over her shoulder. "Strangely, I find that comforting."

A stark silence zipped through the room. It was charged and uncomfortable enough to have him thinking about the big bed right in front of him and Cam squirming as if he wanted to bolt.

He inched toward the door, looking like he was about to do just that. "I should head back to the helicopter and lock it up. Also need to check in with Connor."

Joel nodded. "Fine."

"Who is that?" she asked, seemingly unaware of the firestorm she'd set off in the man she'd once dated.

Joel swallowed a few times and thought about every unsexy thing he could to overwhelm the other thoughts in his head. After a few seconds, his control zapped back to life. "Our boss, Connor Bowen. He runs the Corcoran Team."

"Yeah, like I said, I should contact him." With his hand against the door, Cam appeared to want to do it right then.

Joel didn't disagree. He'd been toying with yelling for the cavalry, but he didn't want to rush everyone in before they conducted a few more easy steps. "Let's see if we can figure this out first. It's still possible we have an annoying businessman acting like a spoiled child."

"How do you explain the gun?" Cam asked.

Joel couldn't. Not without hitting on options that had his temper spiking. That was the problem. "I'm thinking Mark snuck in here and took the box."

"What?" Hope jumped off the bed and wrapped her arms around her body.

"I know that sounds bad, but—"

"While I was sleeping? No way." She rubbed her hands up and down her arms. "Don't you think I'd hear him?"

Cam winced. "Maybe not."

She visibly shivered. "That's just creepy."

"And one of the reasons your dad wanted me here." Joel slid that in there in the hope it would cut off any argument he'd get on the helicopter when they flew out of there the second after they located Mark. Thanks to all she'd described about this retreat so far, he'd leave when she did and not a minute earlier.

She held up a hand. "Don't start."

Looked like her fear or disgust or whatever it was about the lockbox had disappeared. "Your dad is being practical." Joel suspected her father was also engaging in a bit of matchmaking, but Joel decided not to share that thought.

"The word you're looking for is overprotective."

"Hope, I think—"

She turned to Cam. "So, now what?"

He bit his bottom lip in what looked like a poor attempt to block a smile. "We check the helicopter and do a quick search around the campground."

Those priorities worked for Joel. "Cam will question the men here at the campground and maybe see if Charlie knows anything or can give us some direction."

"He knows these woods better than anyone and probably can tell us where someone might hide." She sighed as she shook her head. "I swear if Mark is just being a big baby and staying away because a woman yelled at him, I'm going to hit him."

"Absolutely fine, since nailing him with an arrow is out. Unfortunately," Joel said.

Cam nodded. "Sounds like a reasonable plan."

She let her hand drop to her side again. "But Mark being a jerk still doesn't explain the missing satphone and the stalker."

"You're sure Mark wasn't the one following you?" Man, Joel wanted that to be the answer. It was simple and clean, but he knew life rarely worked that way. Not for him.

"The build was all wrong. Mark is stocky and a bit out of shape. This guy was lean and moved fast."

"I don't like that at all." Cam shook his head as he peeked out the small window next to the cabin's front door. "Heads up—the troops are gathering by the fire pit again. Looks like Charlie is giving them orders."

"I bet Jeff pays attention to Charlie," Hope grumbled.

Cam snorted. "Annoying but at least they're listening. Good to know they can."

Sounded like time had run out. Joel didn't want to spend one more second in planning mode. "Okay, we meet back here in two hours. If we haven't found anything, we start looking in the other cabins."

Hope reached down. "I'll bring—"

No way was Joel dealing with that. "The bow stays here."

"Fine." She got up and joined the men at the door. She glanced at Cam. "I thought you had to be somewhere else today."

He nodded, like he always did. "I'm fine for now."

"Maybe we should all be in on the questioning. I mean, I already checked the woods."

Joel knew that would eat up too much time. "This go-round we'll look for tracks."

"Want me to do that? It's more of my specialty than yours," Cam said.

"We'll be fine."

Cam reached for the doorknob. "I bet."

"Can I have a gun?"

Her question stopped both men. Cam froze and Joel did a quick count to ten. She could handle it, but she was still spooked and he had to be sure she was back in full control before he handed her a loaded gun. Still… "No."

"Can you shoot?" Cam asked.

"Been practicing since I was ten."

Joel wasn't having this conversation right now. He reached around and shoved the door open, bringing the warm breeze inside. "Shooting a person is different."

Her head snapped back. "Are we doing that?"

He hoped not. "Maybe."

"And you would know how hard that is."

He glanced at her over his shoulder. "Yes, I would."

THEY'D CROSSED OUT of sight of the campground before Hope broached the difficult subject. Actually, about a hundred feet away she opened her mouth and then closed it again, focusing on the sway of branches against the increasing wind and the clomp of their feet against the ground.

Later they hit the point where she could see sunlight up ahead and knew the helicopter sat a short distance away. She didn't hold back. "Are we going to talk about it?"

He stopped scanning the trees and large expanse of forest around them to spare her a glance. "About what?"

Men were clueless. "Us."

He exhaled. "Hope—"

"I know. You don't have to list off the reasons why we should pretend we've never slept together."

"I never said that."

"You act like it."

"And, for the record, it was more than sex."

"Was it?" She asked even though she couldn't stand to hear him dismiss their relationship as unimportant—again.

True, they hadn't been together in what felt like forever. She'd convinced herself she didn't care and could move on, but seeing him made her realize how untrue that was.

He picked a leaf off a branch that nearly whacked him in the face. "We can't do this now."

The world around her barely registered. Not when this topic came up.

She'd heard all of the excuses. They ran through her mind on constant play. They spilled out of her now before she could call them back. "This is the wrong time. I'm the wrong guy. You deserve better. My background is a mess. My job is dangerous."

He stopped. "Excuse me?"

"Have you invented more reasons? I've heard all of those, and none of them sent *me* running."

"Wow."

She debated storming ahead, leaving him floundering, but refrained. Childish wasn't the answer when what she really wanted was for him to treat her the way a woman deserved to be treated. "Imagine how I felt as you ticked off that list, or some version of it, day after day. You always had a new reason to push away and leave, but you never found one to stay."

"That's not true."

She knew it was because she had lived it. "All those months ago I asked you to move in with me since you were basically staying there every night anyway, and you flew out of town on a business trip the next morning instead of giving me an answer."

"That was legitimate."

"Joel, come on."

The leaf disappeared as Joel crushed it inside his clenched fist. "Your father said you were dating again."

Her gaze slipped back up to his. "What?"

"No?"

The conversation had her mind spinning. Her dad still talked with Joel? And since when was her dating life up for discussion? Not that she really had one. She struggled through a few setups from friends and had a perfectly nice time with a guy from her climbing club.

Handsome men, fun places and she didn't experience so much as a spark. Not even a tiny nibble of interest.

But that's not where her mind went when Joel asked the question. It zoomed right to her nightmare scenario. The one where he walked away and found someone else. Where the truth turned out to be not that he wasn't ready to make a commitment but that he didn't want to make one to *her*.

"Are *you?*" Two simple words, but it actually hurt her to say them.

"I didn't leave you so I could date other women. My decision wasn't about being a playboy." His voice rose and anger slipped in as he spoke.

As if he had a right to be upset about the fallout. "Well, I guess that's good to know."

Instead of standing around arguing, she headed in the direction of the helicopter. This was a waste of time and they had more important things to worry about than her broken heart.

Joel grabbed her arm before she got more than three feet. "Hey, wait up."

She didn't shake out of his grip, though she could have because his hold was more gentle than confining. Seeing the pain in his dark eyes killed off any thought of pulling back anyway.

He closed in, bringing his body within a few breaths of hers. "You know I'm telling the truth, right?"

"I know you had a lot of excuses. Still do." And she couldn't hear them again. Not and still function.

"Hope, look…I want…"

"What?" She heard the pleading in her voice.

His eyes closed and when they opened again the wary expression hadn't faded. "Maybe we should stick to finding Mark."

Just like that, the mood changed. Something snapped and the tension that had been building blew away.

Because he seemed to want an out, she gave him one. Maybe a change of topic made sense. There had been so much pain and disappointment, so many tears. She needed her head in the game and her mind on Mark. "Fine. Why are we headed back to the helicopter instead of following tracks?"

"I want to check in at work."

"And?" Joel's face went blank and she wasn't falling for it. "Oh, please. Maybe I didn't see you walking out on me, but I do know you. Part of you, and you are fixated and worried."

"I didn't leave you—"

"Joel."

His hand dropped. "Okay, yes. I'm concerned."

"You're admitting it?"

"You deserve that much." He motioned with his head for them to start walking again. "This is your job, and I think something is very wrong here."

The honesty flooded her with relief. "Good."

"Why good?"

"Sharing even that much is a big step for you."

"I thought you'd be happy I left." His voice dropped to a near whisper. "Back then, I mean."

The words stunned her and she stumbled. She stared at him, thinking he had to be playing a sick joke, even though that wasn't his style. But he looked ahead, not even blinking.

"You've got to be kidding." She was about to pull him to a stop when a crack echoed through the trees. Dirt kicked up a few feet away from her, and birds swooped out of the trees in a rush.

"Get down!" His full body smacked into her before he finished talking.

The ground rushed up and she put out a hand to stop the free fall. Her legs twisted with his and the second before she slammed into the ground he turned them.

Landing on his side with a grunt, he absorbed the majority of their combined body weight on his shoulder. His body bounced and she tried to move away and let him brace for impact, but he curled her body into his. Still, the jolt rattled her teeth and she heard him swear under his breath.

She could taste dirt and feel sharp sticks jabbing into her bare legs and ripping off her bandage. Her mind finally focused and the sounds of the forest came rushing back. "Joel—"

"Don't move."

It had sounded like… But it couldn't be. "What was that?" She whispered the question as she frantically looked around.

Before she could scramble to her feet, he shoved her against the ground and covered her body with his. His fingers slipped into her hair as he held her down. She heard a steady stream of reassuring words, but they barely registered over the fear and panic pounding through her.

She expected shouts and more pops. When nothing came, she glanced up. His gaze scanned the area, and his gun was up and ready. She swallowed hard at the vulnerability of their position. Right there on her makeshift path with nothing covering them or blocking their view in any direction.

"A gunshot." He was so close the words vibrated against the side of her head.

Adrenaline pumped through her, and her heartbeat hammered in her ears so loudly she thought for sure she'd give away their position. "Where did it come from?"

"I'm more worried about who and how many." He shifted his weight until most of it fell away to her side. "Stay under me."

"Are you wearing a bulletproof vest?"

"Didn't think I'd need one."

She waited for the attacker to rush them. Listened for another shot. "I can't hear or see anything."

"I need to get to the helicopter."

A vision of him running and getting shot hit her with the force of a crashing train. The horror of it stole her breath and had her fingernails digging into the dirt. "No."

"I have a vest and binoculars in there." He slipped farther off her. "Other weapons."

"You can't risk going into the open."

With barely a touch he moved them to the left. She felt his deep inhale before he rolled them over and stopped close to a large tree trunk. He tapped the back of her legs. "Curl up."

When the world finally stopped spinning she looked up and saw rough bark right in front of her face and threw a hand out to touch the surface. "What are we doing?"

"You are going to make yourself as small as possible." He gave the orders without looking at her. His head kept moving as he glanced around them. "Then you're not to move."

"You can't—"

"I'm serious. You move and I will come back, which is more of a threat to me than racing over there." With a hand between her shoulder blades, he lowered her closer to the ground. "Stay down."

Before she could grab on or call him back, he was gone. In a crouch, zigzagging he broke through the last line of trees. He hugged close to the helicopter as he lifted a hand. The door must have stuck or his angle was off because she saw him pulling and tugging.

With all her concentration, she focused on him. Her teeth clicked together as terror spun through her. She waited for footsteps to fall and a hand to pull her up. The only thing that kept her from screaming was watching Joel. Even as her vision blurred around the edges, she stared.

After some fiddling and a yank, he got the door open and bonelessly slipped inside. One minute his dark hair provided a beacon and the next he was gone.

Her breath hiccupped in her chest as she fought the urge to run after him. She'd just decided to do that when she saw his head again. He held binoculars and swept his gaze over the forest. The door inched open and he was off again, this time running toward her.

He slid in beside her, kicking up twigs and leaves around her. He held up a vest. "Put this on."

"You need it."

"I think the person is gone, but I don't want to risk you getting shot."

When he continued to hold the vest, she took it and slid it on. The way he stared at her with that I-can-wait-all-day expression had her adjusting the straps and securing it tighter to her body. "Happy?"

"Not really."

That made two of them. She looked at the binoculars. They weren't the standard bird watching kind.

"Do they do something special?" She half hoped they functioned as a grenade launcher. She'd be satisfied with any weapon that could protect them all and get them out of there fast.

"Increased magnification and brightness. Plus the universal mil reticle." He spit all that out without lowering the glasses.

"Um, okay."

"The last is a special feature snipers use." This time he looked at her. "It allows for better targeting and range estimates."

The techno-jargon filled her with a strange sense of relief. It was as if they had walked right into his wheelhouse. She was fine to stay there with him.

Despite all their personal troubles, she never doubted his competency on the job. He was the man any sane person would want on her team when things fell apart. Now qualified.

Still, the sniper talk had her attention. "I don't know most of the words you just used."

"It means—"

She put a hand on his arm. "Don't explain. I'm just happy you know what you're talking about."

He nodded. "We need to get back."

The comment started a new round of thundering in her chest. "How do we know it's safe?"

"I'll feel better when we're in the cabins."

She'd feel better in her town house. "Any chance your team is on the way?"

"I called them. Yes."

"That's good news." But she noticed he wasn't smiling and didn't look one ounce more relieved than he was before he crawled into the helicopter for reinforcements. "Right?"

"I'll explain later."

Something inside her shriveled. "I was afraid you'd say that."

Chapter Five

Tony Prather had no idea who or what Connor Bowen was, but the man was on his way up to the executive floor of Baxter Industries. Tony glanced out of his conference room window to the Washington, D.C., skyline in the distance. His Rosslyn office had a view across the Potomac River to Georgetown.

He'd worked hard for his position with the big office, complete with private executive bathroom and two administrative assistants. He wasn't accustomed to jumping when others issued orders. If anyone other than Rafe Algier had phoned in from a trip abroad and asked, Tony would have had someone on his staff offer an excuse and insist he couldn't be disturbed.

But Algier Security had sent work Baxter's way, and back when business was floundering Rafe had provided some much-needed contracts and personnel to help keep Baxter's doors open. Tony had a strong loyalty to the man. It was why he had agreed to hire his daughter for the executive retreat.

Well, part of the reason. Tony didn't get where he was by being soft. His obligation didn't pass from Rafe to his daughter.

Tony had taken over the reins of Baxter after a coup by the old board of directors. When the bottom fell out of the financial markets and business dried up, the old president and chief executive officer lost the confidence of everyone from shareholders to the management staff. Tony stepped in and got the place running again. He expanded the company's services.

They no longer just provided tech and personnel to government agencies. Now his people staffed Fortune 500 companies and smaller businesses. Anyone who didn't want to pay employee benefits and could afford Baxter's bills was welcome.

But that didn't mean he had time to babysit some guy with an agenda. And Rafe hadn't taken the time to explain anything, which ticked Tony off. He had other worries. All his plans, those tenuous pieces he needed to come together and fit just so, were breaking down. He had a partner he didn't trust and a problem he needed to fix.

He'd rebuilt it all and couldn't afford to have it crumble now. Not when he was so close to the end.

The phone on the credenza buzzed and he gave the okay for one of his assistants to usher in their unwanted guest. Better to get it over with and move on.

The man who stepped through the glass doors and stopped was not what Tony expected. Tall with dark hair, he wore a business suit minus the jacket. But that's not what stuck out. It was the lethal look. The man appeared ready for battle. So did the muscled man behind him.

Earlier, Rafe had talked about needing to get in touch with his daughter. Tony had barely listened because the mere mention of Hope Algier's name at this point in the process had Tony speed dialing his partner. Not that he could get through.

"I'm Connor Bowen." The man motioned to the guy with him. "This is Davis Weeks."

"Gentlemen." Tony nodded because that's what protocol demanded.

Inside, his rage boiled. He'd prepared for one of them. Bowen was president and owner of something called the Corcoran Team. The Internet and paperwork trail pointed to a threat assessment group. The kind of team that taught businessmen how not to get kidnapped while playing in Mexico and made plans for getting them out when they did.

All aboveboard and clean, but Tony recognized an off-the-books undercover operation when he saw one. And that had his interest. So did this Weeks character. The guy hadn't blinked and if the bulge under his jacket was an indication, he'd somehow snuck a gun through security.

"I'm Tony Prather." He motioned toward the seats across the conference table from him. "I was told only one of you would be coming."

"Davis is my second in command. He understands the situation."

Because Tony needed to know what that was, he played along. Still, this was his turf, so he took the lead. "What can I help you with?"

Connor leaned forward with his elbows folded on the table in front of him. "There's a problem at your management retreat."

A stark silence followed the statement. Tony guessed that was the point. Drop the bombshell and then assess his reaction.

He had no intention of giving them anything. "Meaning?"

This time Davis spoke up. "One of your executives is missing and there's been some other trouble."

"This is a get-away-from-it-all retreat. How would you

know what's happening there?" Tony had been trying to check in, and the messages he'd received made no sense.

Connor's hand dropped to the table, and his fingers drummed on the top. "Some of my people are there."

The information would have been good to know before now. Funny how Rafe had left that out. "Some?"

"More than one."

The steady thumping touched off a headache. Tony had enough of that right now. "Care to tell me why?"

Connor shrugged. "As a favor to Rafe."

Looked like he wasn't the only one indebted to Rafe Algier in some way. Tony wasn't sure how he felt about that. The idea of the old man moving the chess pieces around, using them all, had Tony balling his hands into fists on his lap.

"Does he know his daughter is tangled up in this?" Tony had put her there for a reason and now it could all unravel thanks to this Corcoran Team and Rafe's meddling.

"Not all the details," Connor said. "Rafe is breaking away from his meetings in Vietnam and should be taking off soon to head back."

"This is that serious?" Tony noticed only the one in charge talked. Tony appreciated the chain of command as much as the next guy, but the silence from Davis proved unnerving. The guy sat and stared.

A lesser man would get twitchy and start talking. If that was the plan, these two sorely underestimated him. Tony Prather could not be intimidated. Others had tried and failed at using that tactic.

He hadn't won his current position by shaking hands and saying yes all the time. He'd pushed his predecessor out and never looked back. He'd won the office and the hot young wife. That's what he did—he won.

Davis finally shifted in his chair. The movement was slight, but it had the focus switching to him. "You didn't ask which executive is missing."

Tony knew all about Mark's situation. Knew and was watching, but these two didn't need that information. "I'm assuming whoever it was got lost on a hike and this isn't really a big deal."

Davis and Connor exchanged glances. Connor started talking again after Davis nodded. "Right before I spoke with one of my team members earlier today, he came under fire."

Tony was more interested in which man was in charge than about this conversation. Still, he had a role to play. "You mean—"

"Gunshots." Connor exhaled as if explaining bored him. "At the camp."

Time for concern. Hitting the appropriate level would be the trick. Tony went with pushing his chair back and reaching for the phone. "I need to get them all out."

"My people are working on that." Connor glanced at the phone and continued when Tony returned it to the cradle. "Once the weather breaks we'll move in."

Not the response Tony had expected. He figured they'd rush in and rescue, or whatever they normally did. The change in expectations and protocol sent a new push of adrenaline rushing through him. "Send in the park rangers. Do something."

Davis's eyes narrowed. "If we didn't have a 'shots fired' situation, maybe, but we can't risk putting anyone else in danger."

All reasonable answers. But Tony couldn't shake the feeling he was being sized up and checked out. That was probably fair because he was playing the same game at the moment.

Right now he needed to know their real plan. He guessed they wouldn't share most of it, but maybe he could drag out something. "So, what's next?"

Connor thumped his fingertips even louder. "My guys will secure the scene until I can get emergency personnel in there."

Tony glanced down but Connor didn't stop. "And in the meantime what happens to my executive?"

"We try to find him," Davis said.

Definitive and solid. Tony looked for a chink in their show and didn't see one. The routine came off as practiced but appropriate. He had to admit a part of him was a little impressed. These two could give lessons in remaining cool and detached.

"Should I contact his family or at least notify the board?" he asked.

"Let's see where we are tomorrow." Connor stood up. "We need to get back, but I'll keep you updated."

"Absolutely." Tony reached across the table and shook their hands. "Thanks for coming in."

Connor nodded. "I'm sorry I don't have more definitive news."

"I'm going to continue to believe this is a case of wandering away from camp and not a disaster."

"Except for the gunshots." Davis delivered the line in a flat voice. He didn't say much, but what he did force out came with a punch.

Tony admired the skill. "That could be hunters, anything."

"I have a conference call scheduled with search and rescue. You're welcome to listen in." Connor slipped a business card out of the pocket of his dress shirt and set it on the table.

Tony left it there. "I appreciate that. My assistant

can give you all my contact information, including the home numbers."

"Good." Connor headed to the door with Davis right behind him.

At the last minute, Davis turned around again. "Mark."

That fast the air sucked out of the room. "Excuse me?"

"Your missing executive. His name is Mark Callah." For the first time, Davis smiled.

Tony found it more intimidating than the staring. "Connor already told me that."

"Did I?" he asked.

Tony stuck with the story because he refused to believe he'd messed up and not asked what would be the obvious question. This was a trap and he would not fall into it. "Yes."

"I'll call in a few hours." After one last up and down, Connor left, taking Davis with him.

Joel tried to think of a way the past hour could have gone worse. Hope wanted to have "the talk" in the middle of a potential missing persons case. Add in bad weather, gunshots and no answers, and Joel wanted to yank all of them out of there and go home.

He might have done so if the flight wasn't dangerous and he didn't have a missing camper lost out in the unforgiving woods somewhere. Still, the idea of shoving Hope on the helicopter and telling Cam to fly her to safety was compelling. The fact that she would refuse wasn't Joel's biggest concern. He could—would—make her if that's what he had to do to keep her safe.

He had left her to give her a normal life. Forfeiting that now was not okay with him. Not after all he'd lost.

They stepped into camp. When Joel saw the flat expression on Cam's face, he knew something was wrong.

"What's going on?" Joel called out.

Cam joined them at the line where the trees met the open space. "Perry's officially missing."

Hope let out a stifled gasp. "You've got to be kidding. We're missing two now?"

"Charlie last saw him in the kitchen area around breakfast, but there's no sign of him at all." Cam kicked the dirt under his feet.

Joel tried to ignore the uncharacteristic shifting, but it made him nervous. "His bed?"

"Slept in and all of his stuff is in his cabin." Cam looked up. "Good news is we don't have blood this time."

"I can't believe that now qualifies as good news." She leaned against Joel.

Cam shrugged. "Well, it's not as bad as it could be."

Without thinking, Joel put a hand against her lower back and brought her in closer to his side. Despite the warm weather, her skin felt cold and the chill seeped through his clothes to his skin. The wind had cooled, but not enough to explain the shivers running through her.

Cam's gaze shot to the lack of space between Joel and Hope, then back up again. "Jeff and Lance are pretty jumpy. Charlie is on the side of that last cabin, walking them through some camping tips."

As far as Joel was concerned, that was the sort of thing that should have happened before the retreat started. "Now?"

"I did that before," she said.

Cam waved off the concern. "I think he's trying to keep them calm."

"Well." Hope rubbed her hands up and down her arms. "Maybe I should listen in then."

Joel knew she was suffering from a case of nerves. She didn't need a class on wilderness survival. In their months apart she'd taken more and more risks, climbing higher mountains and guiding tours thousands of feet into the air. He hated the idea of her up there, but he knew she loved it. And they were no longer together, so he limited his complaints to her dad. Not that they worked.

The corner of Cam's mouth lifted as his gaze wandered over Hope and Joel. "What happened to you two?"

"Get ready for more bad news," she said.

Joel didn't feel like playing games, so he skipped right to it. "Someone shot at us."

Cam's mouth fell into a flat line again. "What?"

She blew out a long, labored breath. "One shot but it had us ducking."

Cam nodded. "I'd think so."

"Well then." She stepped out of Joel's hold. "I should go do some work."

Joel admired her courage to not sit in a corner and rock. Most people would, but not her. But he still worried about her shell-shocked expression and wavering voice. "You okay?"

Cam cut off any chance of getting her to stay. "I need to talk with you."

Even though he wanted to follow her, Joel let Hope go but not before one more reminder. "You need to check your knee and put on another bandage."

She nodded but didn't say anything. That didn't stop him from staring. He watched her walk across the campground, ignoring the gentle swish of her hips and not breaking focus until he saw her stop next to Charlie in the distance.

Cam took a few steps and came to stand beside Joel. "The others were with me the whole time. None of these three could have taken the shot at you."

Joel had already come to that conclusion. Ruling some

people out narrowed their choices. He didn't like any of the remaining ones. "Then we need to deal with the very real possibility either Mark or Perry, or both, are at the bottom or this."

"There's another possibility." Cam matched Joel's stance and stared at the others as well. "We could have an unknown out here stalking people."

There it was. The worst possible answer. An unknown meant they were dealing with a surprise. The person could be on drugs or unstable or just enjoy killing.

Joel didn't want Hope near any of those types. "I've been trying not to think about that option."

"It would explain the gunshots." Cam stared at him then. "I'm guessing you didn't see anyone."

"Nothing. The guy totally got the drop on me."

Cam made a face. "Weird."

"I know." Joel understood the surprise. He wasn't the type to miss someone sneaking up on him.

He'd been training for surveillance his entire life. He had tracked and practiced from the day after he turned seven and his dad insisted the family go totally off the grid. Maybe those early lessons grew out of his father's sick paranoia, but he instilled a sense of caution and taught certain skills. The same skills that served Joel well as he passed from one position to another in the intelligence community.

That likely meant the attacker was equally well trained. Joel hated that prospect.

Cam let out an impressive line of profanity. "What did Connor say?"

"He's on the way and will bring everyone from the forest rangers to the local police with him."

Connor was solid that way. No questions or explanations needed. Joel was on a few days of leave, but he knew if he sent up the red flag, the team would come running.

He'd missed that in his other employment positions and throughout most of his life. He didn't know the sensation of someone putting it all out there for him. His mom had died before he could really know her, and his father's idea of love was handing over a rifle and teaching him to shoot.

Now Joel needed to fill Cam in on the bad part. Joel owed him that since Cam was only out here as a favor. "One problem."

"I'm not sure we need another."

"A storm is moving in."

"Of course it is." Cam groaned. "There's always a storm right when you don't need one."

"Connor can't get in until morning, and even then that's not a guarantee." Joel doubted the timetable anyway. He could smell the rain in the air and feel the dampness on his skin, even though not a single drop had fallen. But Connor talked about violent thunderstorms rolling in and Joel guessed they were headed this way. At the very least, the weather grounded planes. "So, we hunker down."

"I was afraid you were going to say that."

And it was about to get worse, so Joel braced. "I say we do a quick meal, stick together until dark or rain or whatever comes first. Then those of us with weapons split up and bunk with the others."

Cam's mouth broke out into a full grin. "Let me guess which cabin you'll be in."

Knowing the ribbing could go on for hours, Joel ignored the first shot. "You with Lance and we'll let Charlie handle Jeff."

"And you with Hope."

Joel rolled his eyes. "Yes."

"You ready to tell me what happened with her before you came to Corcoran?"

He still battled with the details. He couldn't lay it out there. Not after he was barely holding together from Hope's insistence they pick at it. "No."

Cam nodded and Joel thought he might be in the clear. They needed to concentrate and—

"I'm thinking you'll need practice," Cam said, breaking into Joel's thoughts.

He bit back a groan. "Meaning?"

"I don't know much about women—"

"True."

"—but even I know there's no way you're going to spend the night together without the topic of your relationship implosion coming up." Cam ended the comment with a knowing look.

Joel ignored the description of his upcoming evening, even though he wanted to deny it. "We're grown-ups."

The nodding came back. Cam did love to nod. "I'm guessing that's what she'll say before she demands an explanation."

"What makes you think we didn't work this out already?"

Joel wished. He wanted to fix the damage and move on. Because forgetting her appeared to be out of the question, he'd settle for a healthy parting. One that took away the sadness that moved into her eyes when she talked about them.

"What was the word you used earlier on her?" Cam looked up and closed one eye, as if he were pretending to mull it over. "Oh, right. Experience."

"We're the same age and I doubt you're any better at

this women stuff than I am." Joel hoped for Cam's sake that wasn't true.

"But I wouldn't be dumb enough to let that woman go."

This time Joel nodded. There was that.

Chapter Six

Hope tried busywork to calm the nerves somersaulting in her stomach. With her knee bandaged and everyone tucked away, she tried to settle in. She drew down the bed covers, then drew them up again and tucked them around the pillows.

Next came sitting. She dropped onto the mattress and looked around the cabin. It was a utilitarian space with dark furniture and windows that rattled when a strong gust of air blew in, like right now. Her space measured about twenty square feet more than the others and included an inside shower.

That was pretty much a prerequisite for her on a retreat like this. She'd rather go without than risk flashing half the camp. Here she didn't have to make the choice.

But she had bigger problems ahead. Well, one. Joel.

He stood with his broad back to her and stared out the small window next to the door. He wore the same pants he was wearing when he'd landed. Charlie had lent him a clean T-shirt. The rest of Joel's clothes sat in his bag on the helicopter. He insisted another run was too risky in light of the guy practicing his sniper skills out here.

Rain pelted the windows and had kept them all trapped inside for the past few hours. Now the sun had gone down and the ceiling light in the center of the room highlighted everything, including all six-feet-whatever of him.

The ruffled dark hair and scruff around his chin had always been her favorite look for him. Made him look rugged and reminded her of his sexy ability to handle almost any situation.

"We've slept in the same room before." He made the comment without looking at her.

She had to smile. "Many times, but we were dating back then."

Sometimes she thought the phrase "eyes in the back of his head" was invented to describe him. He always seemed to have a clue about what was happening around him, even if he acted like he didn't care or his eyes were closed.

"True." He turned but didn't move one inch closer. "And no one was shooting at us."

"Now look at us." She sat on her hands to keep from fidgeting or waving them around.

His gaze bounced to her lap, then back to her face. "I'll sleep on the floor."

Interesting how he had his lines and she had hers. Having him nod off during the next shoot-out was not her idea of a good time. "You'll sleep in the bed with me."

"That's not a great idea."

Oh, she knew that. His scent, his arms. The way he wrapped his body around hers and pulled her in tight. All dangerous for her self-control. "Agreed."

He held out a hand. "Then throw me a pillow and—"

"But it's still happening."

With that his arm dropped to his side again. "You go to my head."

And he didn't look particularly happy about the idea.

His face stayed blank and his eyes flat. He froze in place and looked as likely to bolt as he was to take a step closer.

The words both freeing and empty went to her head and stuck there. "What does that mean?"

"I've never been attracted to a woman the way I'm attracted to you." He pushed away from the door and walked across the room.

With each step, his hiking boots fell quietly against the hard floor. The cabin walls creaked and thunder drummed in the distance. The harder the winds and heavier the sheets of rain, the more she waited for the outside to storm in. The sturdy structures held, but a dribble leaked in at the back left corner near the open closet.

All she could focus on was the soft tap of his steps until he stopped in front of her. With only a foot separating them, she could smell him. Feel the weight of his gaze upon her.

As she stood, her gaze traveled over his flat stomach and the smooth muscles under his damp tee. "So, naturally, you left me."

"Normal doesn't work for me."

How many times had she heard that excuse? It appeared to be his favorite, which made it her least. "You say that often enough for it to be your motto."

"The way I was raised…" He broke off and shook his head. "Look, things can work for a little while but that's it."

There it was. The blanket statement that ended it all. The sentiment would have been sweetly misguided if it hadn't driven them apart. He believed. It amounted to nonsense talk, but in his head he viewed it as truth.

Shame that on this one issue he ignored the reality that life could be better than what he was handed. "How do you know?"

His eyes narrowed. "What?"

"How many long-term relationships have you had?" She steeled her body for the verbal blow. She had a theory and put it out there, hoping she'd turn out to be right.

"We should talk about something else." He started to pivot.

"I'll narrow it down for you." She spoke louder and put a hand on his arm to hold him there. "Did you ever live with a woman?"

He blinked a few times. "Just you, and that was informal."

The relief crashing over her nearly knocked her down. "Ever date one woman for more than three months in a row?"

He didn't hesitate. "You."

The last of the tension whooshed out of her. Even though she seemed to be the only one fighting for them, at least he refrained from using her weakness for him against her. "Then you have no idea what you could or couldn't do long term."

"I didn't go to school until I was eleven." He folded his hand over hers where it lay against her arm.

"Do you think that's a test for something?" The rain cast dampness over everything and had her shivering, but his touch sent warmth spiraling through her.

"Yes, for everything."

His palm brought the heat back to her limbs. "All it says to me is your father was a sick man, which I already knew. He grew paranoid and scary and died from a brain tumor. You didn't hide that from me."

His hand squeezed hers. "That wasn't really an option since your father had my information and knew."

Not a surprise. Her father specialized in collecting information. The more confidential and harder to find, the more he liked hunting it down. He was a specific type of person. The same type as Joel.

"Believe it or not, he didn't hand me your personnel file," she said.

This time Joel smiled and life sparked behind those serious eyes. "I bet he tried."

"Yes." He'd lectured, done everything but make a pros and cons list about Joel.

Not that her dad would put anything on the con list. He loved Joel like a son and wanted him to be *the* one for her. Dad had never been subtle on that point.

"Why didn't you take it?" Joel asked.

That was easy. "I wanted to learn everything about you in the *normal* way. Date like normal people. Eat together like normal people. Find out about each other like normal people."

"I remember our first date." His free hand went to her hair. He slid it forward and weaved his fingers through.

"Italian food. We ate for three hours."

He wrapped a lock around his forefinger. "I was done in ten minutes, but I moved a few stray pieces around on my plate because I wanted to be with you as long as possible."

Her heart did a perfect backflip. "When did that stop?"

The sadness moved back into his eyes as his thumb traced her lower lip. "Never."

"So, you left me for a job." The words stuck in her chest, but she shoved them out, letting them rip and tear as they went.

"Yes."

The word hit her like a punch. "And then you left that job for the one you have now."

She didn't understand that choice. He had confessed how much he wanted the position at the Defense Intelligence Agency, how he needed to be available to come and go. That the work would be dangerous and the hours impossible. He'd pick up and leave and couldn't tell her... so they should move on from each other.

The memory of how easy it had been for him to deliver the horrible news still haunted her. She'd begged and he'd walked away. Never looked back.

But now she saw a different man. This Joel didn't celebrate leaving her. When he looked at her he acted as if the need crushed him. She just wished he could see it. She wished he was willing to do something to fix them.

His chest rose and fell on heavy breaths as his fingertips brushed against her cheek. "The DIA job was a mistake."

Not the answer she expected. Not really the question in her mind either. "Was leaving me a mistake?"

He closed his eyes for the briefest of seconds "Hope, don't—"

She stopped his words by putting her palms on either side of his face. "Kiss me."

"No." There was no heat behind the word.

"Why?"

"I won't stop."

She leaned in closer, letting her breath mingle with his. "You will. We'll kiss and then we'll get in that bed and sleep."

"You have more faith in my control than I do."

He acted like this was easy for her. Like she wasn't waging a battle to win *them* back. "You would never touch me without my permission."

"Of course not." His hands went to her waist and with a tug her chest pressed against his.

"You don't have it." She dropped a small kiss on his chin. "You would have to earn it."

"You're killing me." His face went into her hair, and his mouth nuzzled her ear.

The brush of air across her skin sent a tremor racing down her spine. The shiver brought with it an ache. A need to be near him. "That pretty face of yours isn't enough for me to drop my common sense."

He chuckled. "Good to know."

"But you could—"

"Kiss you."

He didn't ask for permission a second time or for an order from her. He dipped his head and his lips touched hers. The kiss slipped from sweet to hot before one second could pass to the next.

Fire rolled over her as her nerve endings sparked to life. Her hands tingled. She wanted to crawl in closer and never let him go.

His mouth passed over hers and a grumble built in the back of his throat. He kissed her hard and deep and kicked life into every fantasy she'd ever had of him, every memory she held as sacred.

When he lifted his head the room continued to spin. Her fingers gripped his back, and her pulse thumped in her ears.

With a groan, he leaned his forehead against hers. "You think we can stop cold after a few more of those?"

She could barely catch her breath. It rushed out of her in huge shuddering gasps. "We're going to stop because we need our rest, although I bet you're going to stay up most of the night keeping watch."

"You do know me." He lifted his head and kissed her again, this one short yet determined.

She pulled her head back before either one of them was tempted to deepen it. "Parts."

He sighed, exhaled, treated her to the whole "you win" vibe males had. "There hasn't been anyone else."

Deep down she knew that. He couldn't look at her the way he did and then run home to someone else. He wasn't that guy. It wasn't his style.

Knowing that and knowing the reality of how people worked were two different things. People moved on. They had sex and fell in love. He was worth it and believed to her soul he eventually would believe it, too. He was a catch, whether or not he realized that.

"But there will be. Someone else, I mean." She whispered the phrase because it hurt to say it louder.

"No."

The quickness of his comeback had the hope inside her surging again. "I'm wondering if you'll ever trust me enough to stay."

He cupped her cheek. "It's not about trust."

That's the part he never got. If he really loved her and trusted her to accept him for who and what he was, he wouldn't run. He'd stay and fight.

But he didn't and she could feel him slipping away again.

She covered his hand with hers and stepped back, breaking the connection between them. "Yeah, it is."

THE CHAIR WITH its thin cushion turned out to be pretty uncomfortable. The longer Joel sat there, the more his lower back ached. But he didn't plan to move. Not when the seat gave him the best view of her on the other side of the cabin.

He'd found a small lamp stuck in the corner. With it plugged in across the room from the bed and the shade turned toward the ceiling, it bathed the cabin in a soft light. Most of the small space stayed hidden in shadows, but he could see her face.

Lying there with his arms wrapped around her and that body pressed against his for hours had amounted to slow torture. Hours with her curled up so close. The position, the smell of her hair, it all brought the memories back.

Eighteen months ago she'd handed him the key to her apartment and temptation pulled at him to stay. He'd wanted to grab it and try to make it work. He'd toyed with the idea even though he always promised himself years ago he would never drag another person into his messed up life.

He'd switched jobs and got antsy. He craved the outdoors and didn't have time for the bar scene. Even now he lived in the third-floor crash pad of the Corcoran Team headquarters instead of taking the time to find his own place.

Committing came hard for him—to a job, to a plan, to a path that got him somewhere other than slinging a gun while hiding in the woods. He didn't want to settle in and act the way other people did.

His time in the DIA ended when his boss accused him of selling the team out for cash. The man pivoted right off the charge, almost immediately, and Joel didn't do anything wrong, but the damage was done in Joel's mind.

He'd spent a lifetime bouncing around from obligation to obligation and hadn't stayed anywhere for long. His upbringing had taught him to keep ties to a minimum and possessions to almost nothing. He'd tried to break the cycle, but since he didn't even have a closet to his name, he'd clearly failed.

Still, the Corcoran Team had changed him, given him focus and a place. Connor set down enough rules to pro-

mote excellence and consistency but didn't microman-
age. That balance let Joel breathe.

In exchange, he filled any role the team needed. He
honed his tech skills to make his work indispensable and
spent hours at the shooting range perfecting his game.
He refused to disappoint the members who had become
closer than family to him.

Then there was Hope. She was everything he wanted.
Smart, athletic, driven and fun. She didn't get caught up
in her father's wealth and wasn't impressed with fancy
cars or the usual trappings. Her one weakness was for
big comfy beds stacked with pillows. He smiled at the
memory of the bedroom in her town house. A man could
fall into it and get lost in the mass of blankets.

Of course, most things about her made him smile. She
didn't pester. She understood the concept of work secrets
and didn't push. Her easy acceptance had almost made it
harder on him. He'd kept waiting for the bottom to drop,
and the tension built with each day it didn't. Another sick
cycle he couldn't figure out how to break.

"I can feel you staring at me." Her sleepy voice floated
through the room.

Even in the limited light he could see her eyes re-
mained shut and her body buried in the covers. She
claimed the whistle of the wind helped her sleep. Could
be, but the humidity hadn't faded and until it did he'd
prefer to sleep without clothing, and that could not happen with her if he hoped to keep his "hands off" promise.

He watched her mouth curve into a smile and tried
to cut off whatever was happening in her head to put it
there. "You should be asleep."

She shifted and made a sexy little grumbling sound.
"With you."

"Being even this close to you is killing me."

Her eyes popped open. "Good."

Funny how she liked that word, especially when she used it for instances he found to be the exact opposite of good. "Why?"

She lifted herself up on her elbow. "You should suffer."

The words stung. They didn't slice through him as they once would have, likely because of her softer delivery this time, but they bit. "Because I hurt you."

She shook her head, and her hair fell over her shoulder. "Because you still are."

Debating how far to go, he decided to give her the truth. Man up and take the deep plunge.

He leaned over and balanced his elbows on his knees. "You know I love you, right?"

"Yes."

Her expression didn't change, but he thought he saw a hint of satisfaction mirrored in her eyes. This woman... "That was easy."

After a sigh, she rolled her eyes. Ran through the entire "men are clueless" list of gestures he'd seen before. "Joel Kidd, nothing about you is easy."

Not really a point he could argue with, so he stuck with rubbing his hands together where they hung between his knees. "Fair enough."

"Come to bed." Her gaze roamed over his tee and down his bare legs.

He wore his boxer briefs and was ten seconds away from stripping them off. Which made his answer very easy. "I should ride out the night over here."

Instead of taking the hint and gathering up the blanket around her again, she threw back the sheet and patted the mattress. "Do it here."

He should have said no. Insisted they'd pushed their

control far enough. He repeated that refrain as he walked across the room and slid in next to her.

The mattress dipped. Before he could think it through, he rolled her to her side and wrapped a hand around her waist. Her back pressed against his chest, and his nose went into her hair. "You feel so good."

She brushed her hand across the arm banding her waist. "Go to sleep."

"I have to go out looking for Perry and Mark tomorrow."

She shifted until her hair hit the pillow and his body hovered over hers. "That's too dangerous."

"It's what I do."

She lifted a hand and skimmed her fingers over his cheek. "You could wait for the rest of your team to arrive."

"Mark and Perry might need help and, if so, the clock would be ticking."

"But you think they're dead."

He hesitated, but her clear eyes had him telling the truth. "That's the worry, yes."

Thundered cracked in the distance and rain pounded the window. Being out in this would be rough on an experienced camper. He doubted two soft businessmen with little experience were faring all that well. Which left Joel with no choice—he had to get out there at sunup.

"I'm going with you."

"Not going to happen," he said in a scratchy voice.

The soft touch of her fingertips against his skin set off a fire inside him. He wanted her, would have been all over her, but he had promised. She'd set down the rules, and he intended to follow them. Even if it killed him, and he was starting to suspect it would.

She lifted her head and treated him to a lingering kiss

before dropping back down again. "Then you really better sleep because tomorrow you'll have a fight on your hands."

The playful side of her...he loved this part. "Is that a threat?"

She winked and flipped over again, facing away from him. "You'll find out in a few hours."

Chapter Seven

The monster thunderstorm moved out, but the rain continued to fall in an annoying drizzle the next morning. The sky turned a hazy gray as the temperature held steady and the humidity rose. Dampness hung on the air and highlighted the smells of the forest. Fresh evergreen and the earthy scent of dirt and grass.

The scene felt familiar and, except for feeling sticky in her clothing, comfortable to Hope. She thrived in this environment. She also had packed the right gear. Sitting on the log turned into a makeshift seat, she wore a rain jacket and kept the hood up, ignoring the pings of raindrops against her face.

She would have stayed inside, where it was safer and certainly drier, and waited for the official breakfast hour to begin, but she had to deal with Joel. More like it, she had to deal with him being gone.

"There he is. Finally." Cam stood over her, staring into the mass of greenery off to the right of the cabins. "He's headed back in."

She could hear the relief in Cam's voice. The same feeling flooded through her. Joel had taken off, without a word to either of them, and headed out to sniper territory. In the world of dumb ideas, that one ranked pretty high up there.

"I should have known he'd skulk off." She blew out a long breath as the anxiety pinging around in her belly slowed. She stretched her legs out in front of her. "He's good at that."

"Not that I know anything about what happened between you two, because I don't." Cam sat down next to her and mimicked her position. "But he's not out in Annapolis partying with other women. I've never even see him checking out the ladies or making moves, and he's had opportunities."

That grumbly sensation came rushing back. "I bet."

"I'm just saying he attracts attention now and then, not that I'd ever admit that in front of him because I'm pretty invested in telling him how he lacks game."

She tried not to smile at that, at all of it. "Sure."

"At least now I know why he keeps the monk's existence."

That part made her beat back a dose of skepticism. Even when they were together she'd see women check him out and look for the chance to make a move. The fit body and hot smile combined with those dark looks and that bit of naughtiness in his eyes. Many women took a second look. He never noticed, that she could tell, but she'd assumed once he was free of their relationship he would. Just one more example of Joel reacting the opposite of how she thought he would.

"In some ways he's really complex—this mass of contradictions and frustrations—and in another he's transparent." Like the part where he ran scared from emotional entanglements. She was far too familiar with that side of him.

"His dad messed him up." Cam shook his head. "I never really saw how much before."

Her gaze snapped away from the man walking toward her and back to Cam. "He told you about his upbringing?"

"The end-of-the-world fears imposed on him. The foster homes. Being separated from his sisters and never truly reconnecting with them again." Cam whistled. "Sometimes I'm amazed he can function, that he's as normal as he is. Don't tell him I admitted that either."

Joel's openness with Cam stunned her. Joel never hid his background or shied away from using his survival skills, but the idea of him talking it out with Cam was a surprise. She liked that Joel had someone close enough, and now she knew Cam wasn't just some random work friend.

But he'd used the magic word. The same one Joel loved to throw around. "That's the problem."

Cam frowned. "You lost me."

Through the dripping of the rain and soaking of the ground, Joel broke through the tree line. His footsteps hesitated for a second, and then he made a beeline for them.

She lowered her voice. "He thinks he can never be normal."

"Then he needs a good kick in the—"

"What are you two doing out here? You shouldn't be in the open." Joel stopped right by her feet. The scowl stayed as he scanned the area around them.

"We were waiting for you to wander back in," Cam said.

"I walked out a few hundred feet and did a perimeter check." Joel turned in a semicircle as his hand traced the trail through the air.

He acted like leaving was no big deal if he was the one doing it. He wasn't wearing a jacket and his shirt was soaked clear through. Never mind the fact there was some guy sitting out there waiting to shoot at them again. "Good thing a bullet can't reach that far."

"I was fine."

She rolled her eyes as she wondered how he would react if the roles were reversed. "This time."

Shuffling started behind her, then she heard footsteps and the low mumble of male voices. Following Joel's gaze, she watched Lance and Jeff walk out to the fire pit area. Apparently no one wanted to stay inside where it was safer.

It wasn't exactly easy to take the two businessmen seriously with the drawstrings pulled tight on their hoods so only a fraction of their faces stood out. They acted as if acid fell from the sky.

She bit back a joke as she stood up, doubting Jeff would appreciate the humor. He'd dragged designer gear with him, most of which was more suitable for Himalayan climbing than camping in cabins.

Amateurs.

Joel nodded to the new members of the group. "Good morning."

"Where's Charlie?" she asked.

He popped up in the distance over Jeff's shoulder a second later carrying a steaming mug of something. "Breakfast is almost ready."

"Forget that." Jeff frowned at all of them. "What's the plan?"

Joel didn't move. "Survival."

One second he stood there alone. The next, Cam got up and took the place beside Joel. Together they formed a wall of lethal males.

Not that everyone got the message or understood the peril. Jeff sent Joel a withering look, one that probably worked when he tried intimidating his assistants. "I'm serious."

"So am I," Joel shot back.

Jeff dragged a foot through the mud before balancing it on the edge of the log. Never mind that people sat there. "Your timing is interesting."

Hope felt the conversation sliding sideways. Whatever point Jeff was trying to make had tension pounding harder than last night's thunder. He kept poking the bear and sooner or later, Joel would unleash. He had the skills to make Jeff look like an idiot, and she feared that showdown inched ever closer.

"What are you talking about?" Joel asked as he spread his stance and folded his arms behind him.

"You two show up and Mark disappears. Now you claim to have heard gunfire."

Joel's eyebrow lifted. "Claim?"

Enough testosterone-fueled nonsense. She stepped in. "It happened. I was there."

Jeff didn't even spare her a glance. "I'm just saying there are easier ways to get a woman into bed."

Joel took a threatening step forward. "That's enough." Only Cam's arm held him back.

"You're out of line, Jeff. Apologize," Charlie said at the same time.

But Jeff wasn't done. Clearly warming up to his theory, he stood taller and crossed his arms in front of him. "Maybe Mark snuck up on you? Maybe he was in the way? After all, the fight between Mark and Hope was explosive. Made me wonder if there was something behind all that anger."

She was two seconds from kicking the guy in the shin. "You should stop talking."

Joel nodded. "Listen to the lady."

Jeff threw his arms wide. "You going to make me?"

"Damn, you're stupid." Cam shook his head as he mumbled.

"Oh, really?"

Before Jeff could move, Charlie clamped a hand on his shoulder. "Sit."

Jeff shirked it off. "Why should I listen to you?"

"Because it's obvious Joel could take you out in a second, and I know the truth." Charlie took a long sip, drawing out the moment. "You and Mark had quite the argument after the gun incident."

Now, there was news that would have been helpful yesterday. Could have lessened some of her guilt, too. Confiscating the weapon had been the right answer, but doubts had bombarded her ever since. Maybe she could have been less firm about it or taken him aside. She'd always found that a show of strength cut down on some idiocy, but maybe she'd miscalculated this time.

"About what?" she asked, not trying to keep the seething anger out of her voice.

"Nothing you need to worry about." Jeff stepped back, separating himself from the group as he glanced around like a cornered animal. "This is insane. Charlie is just protecting her."

"My name is Hope." The guy was just not getting it. His coworkers were missing. This was not some game. "And what fight?"

Charlie shrugged. "I couldn't hear, but there was a lot of pushing and shouting."

Lance had stayed quiet, just watching and frowning. Now he moved, shoving a hand against Jeff's chest. "About what?"

"Don't touch me."

The more the minutes passed, the less Hope liked Jeff.

He acted entitled and childish, and because neither Cam nor Joel looked ready to step in.

She did. "Boys, knock it off."

The shots rang out as she said the last word. Through the misty air and steady wind, the pings echoed.

"Everybody get down!" Joel yelled the order as he made a dive for Hope.

Lance beat him to it. He knocked into her stomach and they both went flying. She hit the ground hard, making a breath hiccup in her lungs. Knowing she had to move, she scrambled up and crawled on her knees and elbows to the log and tried to lie flat behind it.

Lance half covered her as he reached up and tugged on Jeff's sleeve, breaking the spell that had frozen him in place and dragging him down in the mud beside them. Gunfire rang out. Glass shattered somewhere behind her and pieces of wood kicked up when a bullet slammed into the log right by her head.

She heard shouting and scuffling. The sharp smell of gunfire hit her, and a smoky haze filled the air.

Then Joel was there beside her. After a quick look up and down her torso, he and Cam crouched like a protective shield around the group. All but Charlie, who took off for the cabins behind them.

Noises blurred together and crescendoed to a rolling thunder. Everything seemed to rattle as her stomach rolled.

To steady her body, she reached forward and put her palm against the back of Joel's shirt. She wanted to pull him down and out of target range but settled for the touch. Anything to keep the contact.

In a blink it all stopped. No more loud banging and constant movements. Silence fell over them.

The wind blew and branches shifted. But the roar of

noise that filled her ears ceased. Her hand clenched in Joel's shirt as the world came rushing back to her. She could make out Lance's heavy breathing as his weight fell against her. Jeff's whimpering sounded in the background. At least he'd stopped screaming his wife's name.

She heard the crunch of metal and looked behind her. Charlie stood on the cabin porch, half behind a post, with a shotgun in his hands. She had no idea where that had come from.

"Okay, let's double-time this before our friend comes back." Joel shifted around in his position, his gaze taking in the huddle of people behind him. "We need to get everyone inside."

Cam nodded as he came around the far end of the log and pulled Jeff to his feet. "Go right into Hope's cabin. Do not stop or hesitate."

An eerie quiet whispered through the trees. It made her want to bolt for the indoors. Sitting up proved impossible with Lance pinning her leg to the ground.

"We need to go." She pushed against his shoulder, trying to get him to pull out of his ducking position, but he didn't move. "It's okay now. You can move."

Joel stood watch. "Cam, get them inside now."

A new sensation stabbed at her. One of pure panic. The type that had something twisting in her gut. "Lance?"

The tone must have caught Joel's attention because his sweeping gaze landed on her. "What's wrong?"

She put a hand on Lance's shoulder and shook. Still nothing. Pulling it back, she saw the red.

The color drained right out of her as she looked up at Joel. "Blood."

TONY HADN'T ENJOYED his first conversation with Connor Bowen and didn't relish a second one. From the time the man left the office yesterday until this morning, Tony had conducted an impromptu investigation.

It paid to know the man on the other side of the conference room table and be ready for anything. Tony always was, but he hadn't counted on this guy. He expected Hope to be connected, thanks to her father, but word was her life focused on climbing and, now that she'd messed up that career, she was floundering.

That had proved to be only part of the story. Looked like she knew powerful men in dangerous places. Men who didn't know when to back off.

Connor and his team worked in the intelligence field, and his record possessed the shiny, perfect look that came with false IDs. Tony would bet they dealt in hush-hush projects. That made Connor and anyone who worked for him a huge liability.

Tony stared at his closed office door and reasoned out his next steps. He'd worked too long and too hard to get to this uncertain place.

He'd earned his reputation for being ruthless the honest way. He'd move into a company and cut staff and streamline costs and personnel, rarely getting the credit he deserved. The career had him relocating and trading positions while trying to make a series of corporate boards happy.

But this position was his ticket. Show the right numbers and growth, and the big desk would stay his. He would be in charge and the impressive paycheck and windfall bonuses would come his way.

With one sharp knock, his office door opened. So much for his crack staff and the security measures he'd put in place to keep anyone from getting into his office without permission. Connor somehow broke through the protocol after one visit to the place.

That meant one thing: Tony had to get the pseudo-detective out of his business and off his trail. Fast.

He didn't give Connor the satisfaction of mentioning the unapproved entrance. "You're back."

Connor didn't bother with small talk. He walked right across the large office to stand in front of Tony's desk. "I have a few questions."

Not that Tony had any intention of answering them. "Where's your assistant?"

"Second in command."

He leaned back in his chair and slid his palms over the smooth leather of the armrests. "Is there a difference?"

Connor took a quick look around the office. His gaze roamed but he didn't move. "Davis is back at the office, working on this case."

"Case?"

"Yes."

"Exactly how long are you in town?" The man needed to head back to Annapolis and stay there. Tony was half ready to throw him in a cab to make it happen.

"For as long as it takes."

"Interesting response."

Connor's stance relaxed from attack mode to soon-to-attack. The dark suit didn't fool Tony. He knew a fellow fighter when he saw one. This man could ruin everything. He would dig and push, and those were the two things Tony could not afford to have happen.

Without being asked, Connor launched into whatever he came to say. "I thought you could give me some intel on your officers."

The man had guts. Tony had to give him that, but the request, if that's what it was, would never happen. "Intel?"

"Who, what, backgrounds. Personality types." Other

than blinking, Connor still didn't move. "Likelihood for trouble."

Tony tapped his fingers against the end of the armrest. He aimed for mild disinterest. Inside his mind was spinning with ways to end the conversation. "This is starting to sound a bit like an interrogation."

"If it helps you to think of it that way, I'm good with that." The flat tone only added to the feeling of menace.

"It's also a clear case of overreaching."

"Your executive *is* missing."

And what a mess that had turned out to be. "I let you get me upset last time, but this is nothing. Mark wandered away from camp. That's hardly a reason to dig around in people's personal lives."

Connor's eyes narrowed a fraction. "Why do you say that?"

"Because it's not your business where they—"

"I meant the part about Mark. Why do you think he walked off?"

"It's the most logical explanation." That was the story. That was the plan. Simple and straightforward. Except for the part where it all blew apart and now Tony had to deal with bad weather, Rafe screaming on the phone from thousands of miles away about his baby girl's safety and the man across the desk who wanted to rush in and save everyone.

"I told you there were gunshots."

"I doubt it," Tony said. "If that were true, if there were really trouble, the police, park rangers and everyone else would be out there. I'd be getting calls and this would be on the news. You see, Mr. Bowen—"

"Connor is fine."

"Conner then." Though Tony would prefer not to get

so personal. "I turned this company around by being patient. I don't run off or act in panic mode."

"You think I do?"

"Technically, isn't other people's panic your business?" Tony continued to drum his fingers. With each tap he inhaled, trying to slow down his pounding heart and keep his breathing under control. There was no need to show weakness. "Look, Mark likes to show off. He wasn't thrilled with the idea of a young woman running the retreat."

"How evolved of him."

Little did Connor know the woman, Hope, had been a vital part of the plan. Talk about a miscalculation. "My guess is his male ego got wounded and now he's stuck trying to find a reasonable way to save face and come back to camp."

"Is that it?"

"Excuse me?"

"Are you done?" This time Connor moved. He leaned forward with his fists on the far edge of Tony's desk and kept the eye contact locked on him. "If so, let me tell you about my men. They don't panic. They also know what gunfire sounds like because they're experts at rescuing. When they issue a warning it's because something is seriously wrong."

"So you're impressed with your men." By the time he finished, the words rang out in the room. It took all of Tony's control to keep his expression blank and not shift in his chair. "Your point is?"

Connor pushed up and stood straight again. "I take off as soon as the weather clears."

"This is a waste of time and money."

"Possibly, but it's my time and my money to waste."

"Not really since it's my men out there on the re-

treat." Tony needed to bring them in clean and without
them being subjected to questioning. Not unless he could
control it, and he knew Connor wouldn't let that happen
"My suggestion would be to let this play out. I paid for
a certain number of days and want those men out there,
including Mark, who will show up soon, in the woods,
building rapport as promised."

"While getting shot at."

"I think we've discussed that issue enough." Until
Tony knew more about the who and why of the gunshots,
he pivoted around the topic.

"I agree."

Forget relief. Anxiety smacked into him. "You're still
going."

"I'm getting my people out."

That superman complex was going to ruin everything.
Tony sensed it. "I guess that's your choice."

Connor nodded. "I'll let you know what Mark says."

"Meaning?"

"When I find him, I'll get him to talk. Because, *Tony,*
I will find him. That's what I do."

Chapter Eight

Hope stood behind Cam and looked out the small window next to her cabin door. The rainy gray sky beyond didn't provide much light, so they had to rely on a few dull bulbs.

The small space was lined wall to wall with mud-soaked men. The mixed scent of wet clothes and stale air in the confined room gave it the feel of a locker room, though he'd smelled worse, but for her this couldn't be good.

After the frantic racing around outside and piling inside the cabin, Joel could finally breathe. Hearing the familiar crack and watching Hope fall had taken a good twenty years off his life. When she'd moved and Lance had covered her, Joel forced his mind on the attacker, but the twisting-gut fear about her getting hurt had kept him off his game.

Somehow they'd made it with minimal injuries. Hers being the biggest cabin and having the only indoor shower, it won as the staging area—a good place to regroup and plan. And in Lance's case, receive medical treatment.

Charlie was in the other room now while Jeff paced outside the door. Joel had ordered they all rotate in the bathroom and then put on dry clothes. He had enough to worry about without having someone get deathly ill, and he was willing to do anything to keep Jeff occupied. The man was walking around in circles mumbling about finding a new job.

Now Joel hovered over Lance where he sat on the arm of the couch. The stitching would have been done five minutes ago if the guy would stop jerking and hissing. You'd think he'd never been injured before.

Sure, the shot was a bit more than a flesh wound, but not much more. They all had scrapes and bruises, but Lance delivered most of the flinching. How he'd ever made it through his wife giving birth was a mystery.

With one last stitch, Joel dropped a bloody bandage in the small trash can by his feet. He kept up a running dialogue with Lance, thinking it might calm the man down. "You got lucky."

Lance winced as Joel wrapped a clean bandage around his upper arm. "We might have different definitions of that word."

"I'm not even going to mention that you passed out from a puny shot in the arm." Okay, maybe he'd mention it that one time, but now he'd stop.

"I thought I was dead."

Joel had worried a bullet hit Hope, and the punch of pain had nearly knocked him over. Although he didn't want anyone hurt, he wasn't upset Lance had caught it instead.

He was about to thank him for trying to protect Hope, but she broke in. "There isn't a special prize for the least amount of tears when shot."

"I didn't cry." Lance's voice rose as if swearing under his breath didn't telegraph his disgust for the suggestion.

"Because you were unconscious," Cam said without ending his surveillance on the world outside the cabin.

Joel chuckled. He could go a lifetime without seeing whiny Jeff again, but Joel liked Lance. Charlie, now, he was an enigma. Joel had no idea what to think about that guy.

When Lance glanced down at the white bandage and the line of red seeping through, the color left his face. Joel rushed to reassure him. It was either that or risk having the guy pass out again. "The bullet went through and didn't knick anything important."

"It hurts like a—"

"I have some painkillers," Hope broke in as she left her position by the window and squatted down to drag a bag out from under the bed.

"That would be good." Joel pointed at Jeff. "You're next."

The guy stopped mid-pace. "I wasn't hit."

"I meant answers."

Hope frowned at Joel. Took a second and shot most of the men in the room a frown, even Cam, and he wasn't looking at her. "Now might not be the time for a chat."

This topic was not up for debate. Joel's patience had expired. So had his willingness to sit around and wait to become a target. "Someone is shooting at us and we have two unskilled men missing in this miserable weather. So if Jeff here knows something, it's time to speak up."

"I don't."

Hope got to her feet and grabbed a water bottle on her way over to Lance. Her gaze never left Jeff. "Why did you fight with Mark?"

"It has nothing to do with…" Jeff exhaled as he ran a hand through his wet hair. "Look, it was a work issue."

That got Lance's attention. "What was it?"

Whatever Jeff heard in Lance's voice or saw on his

face had his shoulders slumping. "He had these private meetings with Tony—"

"Who?" Cam asked.

"Tony Prather, Baxter's CEO." Jeff kept up the steady stream of sighing. "It felt like Mark was making a play. Going around my back."

"Doesn't Mark rank above you in the corporate scheme?" Hope asked. "He's the vice president, not you."

Leave it to her to point that out. Joel wished he had. "Exactly my question. Jeff?"

"I had some ideas about positioning the company moving forward. One of the divisions had a down quarter but seemed to be bouncing back, and I wanted to capitalize on the upswing." Jeff leaned against the wall and let his head fall back. "I give Mark some notes, he studies them and all of a sudden he's having private meetings with our boss."

Joel could see it all playing out. Jeff, with his oversized ego, wouldn't accept being pushed out. He'd want every ounce of credit he could squeeze out of an idea. "That ticked you off."

Jeff looked around the room. "Wouldn't it do the same to you?"

"Don't know since I've never worked in an office," Cam said.

Joel reached into the specialized first aid kit for another bandage roll as he turned over Jeff's comments in his mind. The man had just handed them a motive. Not a compelling reason to kill in Joel's view, but for Jeff's type it could be. Always looking for an angle, expecting to rise in the ranks at record speed, wanting the perks and big title. Watching someone grab that away could be a brutal ego blow for someone like Jeff.

Reading people was not his strength. Joel glanced at

Hope, looking for her take on the situation. She had good instincts. But because she stood right at Cam's shoulder, looking out the window instead of at Jeff, Joel couldn't tell what she was thinking.

Now Joel wanted to know what had caught her attention and held it so long. "Cam, can you take over for a second?"

"Sure."

The men passed each other in the middle of the room, exchanging gun for bandage. By the time Joel got to the window, Hope stood right in front of it. Talk about becoming a target. With her damp, freshly showered hair pulled in a ponytail and clean white shirt, she stuck out among the group.

Without making a big deal of it, he shifted her out of the direct firing line through the window and lowered his voice. "You okay?"

"You're very handy with a first aid kit."

He noticed she skipped his question, but he decided to let it slide. "One of the many skills demanded by my father."

"He brought about so much bad, but every now and then there's something positive."

"I think you're reaching for a silver lining."

Joel remembered every minute of the last day as a family—protective services ripping his sisters away, the standoff with the police, the shot his dad fired that finally landed him in jail—so he knew the truth. Nothing good happened. Joel couldn't point to one decent thing about the way he grew up either before or after the final takedown of the Kidd family.

She bit her lower lip. "I keep hoping to find something positive about your upbringing."

"That's not an easy task."

She clearly tried to get it. She listened and shook her head at all the right places.

The pain in her eyes as he relayed the facts, some of them anyway, was genuine. It bordered on pity, and Joel hated that. Knew it was human nature but still despised it. Connor and Cam and the few other people in his life who knew bits and pieces also tried to reason it out, but Joel knew that without living it you could never really understand.

Hope had grown up in a loving home with a father who doted on her. Not every day was easy, of course. She'd lost her mother to cancer when she was a young girl, but Hope never worried about having food or running a drill about how to escape the police. She loved her dad. Joel had seen the bond. It bordered on overprotective, but it beat strong.

"I assure you that if Dad had known I would use my abilities to work for any government agency or a team that helps governments, he likely would have shot me on the spot." That was the threat—*disappoint me and you're dead*.

Hope froze. "Why do I think you're not kidding?"

"If only." She'd moved in closer, which put her head back in the line of fire, so he shifted her to the side again. "You need to stand away from the window."

She looked at him and then to that spot outside that seemed to capture her attention. Through the driving rain and storm that had whipped up right when it looked as if it would taper off, she'd focused in on that area.

"What is it?" he asked.

"You know about trajectories, right?"

If this had anything to do with his dad, Joel lost the track on how. "Sure."

"One of the ways I perfected my aim in archery was

to track the trajectory of my arrow. First I played with my stance and did all this math to figure out the proper draw length, and then I got this fancy computer program. Point is, I figured out I was starting out too high and then the drop off…" She smiled. "You should see your face."

"You have to admit this is an odd conversation in light of being trapped in a cabin and all." He put his body in front of her and brought up the binoculars to scan the area.

"True, but the bottom line is Lance's entry wound is higher than the exit." She drew a diagram in the condensation on the window. "I felt Lance get shot. We were on the ground and the bullet came from above, so the angle isn't a surprise, but it's off."

Something had clicked together in her mind. He could see the light go on and hear the growing excitement in her voice. The energy bouncing off her was contagious.

But he still wasn't sure about her point. "That leads you to believe what?"

"I think the shots came not just from someone standing above Lance but from someone in the trees. The trajectory is that steep."

The comment hung there. Even Cam looked up from finishing off Lance's arm. Jeff was the only one who'd missed the discussion. He was too busy trading places with Charlie as he came out of the bathroom in a set of clean clothes that looked exactly like the dirty ones he had just shed.

Hope's intelligence focused all the pieces. As usual, she found a way through the confusion and came up with a reasonable explanation. She was smart and sharp and didn't hide it.

He loved that about her. Of course, he loved pretty much everything about her.

Still, he wanted to make sure they were on the same page. "So you're saying this guy is sitting up in a branch shooting?"

"I think it's a good possibility the shots came from there, but that doesn't answer every question."

"Okay."

"If I'm right about the position, the shooter should have been able to pick us off one by one because we were all truly vulnerable." She stabbed her finger against points in the diagram on the glass. "That leaves us with a bigger problem."

That's what they needed. More problems. "Which is?"

"Neither Perry nor Mark is the athletic scaling-trees type."

Joel hadn't met either man, but he totally trusted her view on this. He could climb and she could probably do it faster than he could, and that was saying something. That didn't mean two businessmen who spent most of their time sitting behind desks had a chance at getting up there. There was a slight possibility that one of them, or one of the men in the cabin, pretended to be clueless and really had sniper tree-climbing skills, but Joel doubted it.

"We're talking some random guy out here shooting for fun." Joel glanced at Cam. His grim expression mirrored Joel's thoughts—that was the absolute worst case scenario. A pure risk and someone they couldn't get a handle on.

Lance made a strangled sound but didn't say anything.

"Unfortunately, the theory leads to more questions. I mean, how would the random guy get down without you or Cam seeing him?" She pointed to the open space outside as she asked.

Joel had that exact question. There were possible explanations, but none of them proved all that convincing.

Cam and Joel were trained. They were on high alert. Even as worrying about Hope getting hurt occupied part of Joel's mind, Cam stayed fully focused.

"It was raining and we were being shot at," Cam said from across the room.

"And you stood out there like a human shield." Hope stopped whispering and went back to her normal voice. "All I'm saying is if someone wanted to kill you, someone with the level of skill to balance in a tree with a gun and then sneak away unseen by two covert agents, he would have killed you."

Charlie stopped running the towel over his wet hair. "What are you guys talking about?"

Hope ignored the older man and talked to Joel. "All the advantage goes to the person in that position. If that were you, you'd hit the target without trouble."

"So would you." Joel knew that was true because she was the most competent woman he'd ever met.

"Where does that leave us?" Cam asked.

Joel fought the temptation to handle the issue now. He just needed the weather to give him a five-minute shot at testing her theory. "With lots of questions and something to do as soon as the storm breaks."

Her eyes narrowed. "Which is?"

"Go out there and look around."

Two hours later the rain had morphed into a steady fall, but the dark sky gave way to white and the wind died down. While Charlie watched from the porch with a gun in his hand, Hope ventured outside with Cam and Joel.

They fought to have her stay behind, but she refused. Because she threatened to follow them the minute they stepped outside, they gave in and brought her along.

They trudged along on either side of her until they

walked a few feet into the wooded area and well within shouting distance of the cabins. Both men had guns and she carried the binoculars but had a gun and her knife within grabbing range.

Cam shifted into the lead as they got close to the tree they'd staked out as the best contender for climbing. "Remind me again why we're doing this?"

"A hunch." That's all she had, but she'd calculated all the angles and run through all the alternatives, and this was the only one that made sense.

"Seems like a dangerous hunch."

"Not if Hope is right." They stopped at the tree and Joel tapped his palm against the bark.

"Which is why I get to be out here, too." No matter what they thought, she didn't plan to stand around and watch. "I'll climb."

Joel snorted. "No way."

"You two are better to guard and I can—"

Joel broke her concentration when he snatched the binoculars and flung them around his neck. Next came the standing jump where he grabbed the lowest branch, which wasn't all that low. The move stretched him out and had his T-shirt riding up and showing off his flat stomach. With an impressive pull-up, he was up and gone in a matter of seconds, leaving her sputtering.

Cam laughed. "He's fast when he wants to be. He's also smart enough to know you're likely better at that than he is and he had to beat you to the punch."

Joel's voice reached them from above. "Maybe less talking since we could be wrong about this and have a guy stalking us even now."

That reality check had her back teeth knocking together. She'd pushed the fear out, insisting she could handle this…somehow.

With that warning, Cam backed her up against the tree and put his body in front of hers until no part of her was exposed. The bulletproof vest Joel made her wear before he opened the cabin door gave her added protection.

If someone came shooting, Cam would go down and she'd have a shot. The mere idea of that had her stomach flipping around.

She cleared her voice and looked up. Beads of rain fell, hitting her face and running under her hood and into her hair. "See anything?"

From this position she spied a flash of blue jeans and the bottom of Joel's hiking boots. His voice sounded distant and the rain muffled every sound.

"It would help if it stopped pouring." That grumble came through loud and clear.

Cam kept watch as his back pressed into her chest. "Take that up with another department."

Joel shifted and she could make him out as he balanced on a branch. He faced deeper into the woods.

She pushed the panic out of her mind. Others might wobble or slide off. Not Joel. He could probably live up there if he had to.

His arms went up and she knew he was taking a look around. "I want a pair of those binoculars."

"We'll get you a pair," Cam said.

"Hold on," Joel called out.

"What?" She looked up and Cam joined her.

"There's something in the trees about thirty feet out."

Hope's body threatened to break into a full shake. She clenched her hands into fists to keep from fidgeting and shifting around. "A person?"

"A rigging of some kind."

She shook her head as the constant thudding of rain

against her jacket had her talking louder. "I don't even know what that means."

"A platform and a gun set-up to fire either at specific times or via remote." Cam spared her a quick look before he went back to checking out the area around them. "A human might not be pulling the trigger now, but a human built the rigging."

"So we're back to everyone being a suspect." She didn't know if that was good or bad. With the businessmen as suspects she at least knew something about her potential attacker.

A rogue sniper terrified her. That suggested someone with skill and put Joel and Cam at greater risk because she knew they would shield the rest of them with their bodies if it came to that. The thought of watching Joel go down almost drove her to her knees.

"Move." A loud whoosh followed the warning. Joel shouted as he dropped out of the branches and landed with a slight bend of his knees as if he'd been practicing the move his entire life.

She heard a thud and saw the binoculars land in the mud. Adrenaline pumped through her as she spun around, looking for the danger that had set him off.

The forest blurred in front of her. Joel grabbed Cam's shoulder and turned him toward the cabins while Joel shoved her behind him and brought up his gun. The men took up positions behind two trunks and faced in the same direction, this time toward camp.

Despite the dizzying few seconds, she stayed locked behind Joel with her fingers slipped through his belt loop.

"Hands up," Joel yelled in the direction off to the side of the far cabin.

She peeked around his shoulder and saw trees and branches and sheets of water. Nothing moved and no sound came. She was about to ask what was happening when a smaller tree bent. The wind didn't take this one. A shadow moved.

"Come out or we fire." Joel pushed her deeper behind the tree as he motioned for Cam to take the far side. "You have three seconds."

She shifted and looked out from the other side of the tree. Then she saw it. The shadow, clearly a large figure, stumbled. "Joel, I think—"

"One..."

"An animal maybe?" Cam asked.

"Two."

Without a sound, the figure dropped. A man's torso fell into the clearing with the rest left behind in the woods. Arms outstretched and a familiar green polo shirt. The rain pounded his face, which was turned toward them.

She started to rush out, but Joel caught her arm. "Wait."

Cam's shoulders fell as he lowered the weapon. "What the—"

But she knew exactly who it was. "It's Perry."

Chapter Nine

They'd informally shared her town house and slept together more times than he could count, but when he
stepped into Hope's confining cabin that night he still
felt about three sizes too big. "At least it smells better in
here than it did ten minutes ago."

She glanced over at him and smiled. "Who knew a
candle could help that much?"

The men had cleared out, with Charlie taking the cabin
on one side of hers and dragging Lance and Jeff along
with him. Cam was looking after their newest patient,
Perry, next door while keeping the first watch on the
camp.

The man hadn't roused long enough to answer even
one question. The nasty gash on the back of his head
suggested a fall or a hit. Joel was betting on the latter.

They had gotten it bandaged, and Cam had agreed
to wake him up in a few hours for a concussion check.
Other than that, all they knew was Perry had the same
clothes on when he stumbled back into camp that he had
worn the night of Mark's fight with Hope.

Every time Joel started to think they'd all walked into
some big work argument between Perry and Mark, the
reality of that gun rigging would strike. Joel just couldn't
see either man having the skills for that, never mind

the equipment. Hope said she had done a bag check… of course, Mark got a gun through, so maybe it wasn't impossible.

Joel took one last sweeping look out the door, then shut it behind him. The rain still fell, but the wind no longer whipped through the trees. He toyed with the idea of loading everyone up and heading for the helicopter, but the darkness and memory of the uneven ground stopped him. Last thing they needed was another injury.

"Still nothing from Perry?" She wadded the old sheet and blanket into a ball and threw them on the floor.

"He's out cold." Trying hard not to think of the bed and her in it, and failing miserably, Joel walked to the farthest point from her.

He should help her strip and remake the bed after they'd laid Perry out there. His clothes had been caked with mud and his shirt soaked with blood. But that side of the room spelled trouble. Even with the danger spinning around them, Joel wanted her and his self-control was going down for the count.

She froze in the act of unzipping her sleeping bag and spreading it over the bare mattress. "Any chance we could lose him during the night?"

Joel decided to go with the least panicked version. "Cam is staying with Perry. We're worried about a concussion. His head is pretty banged up."

"Maybe he got lost and the exposure—"

"No." Joel couldn't let her think that. Not when he needed her on guard for the worst-case scenario. "Something slammed into his head. Either he fell or he got hit."

Her expression hardened. "Where's Jeff right now?"

"Jeff, Charlie and Lance are bunking together." Joel understood her narrow-eyed reaction because he also had suspicions about Jeff. Though the evidence pointed toward Mark as the attacker, something wasn't right with Jeff. Something Joel couldn't nail down. "I want someone with weapons knowledge in each cabin. I don't know if I can trust Charlie, but I trust him more than Jeff."

She dropped onto the bed and balanced a hand on the mattress on either side of her trim hips. "When can we leave?"

This he could handle. Simple emotionless conversation. Joel didn't like the idea of Lance and Perry being hurt or Mark being on the loose, but getting them out of there alive gave Joel something to concentrate on... instead of thinking about her. "I'm not sure if we can move Perry. Without medical help, I can't really assess how bad off he is, and I don't want to drag him around and cause more damage."

"So we're going to live here now?"

"Hardly." Joel bit back the wave of heat hitting him. She sat there in thin sweats and an even thinner tee, looking vulnerable, and his mind started flipping back to them as a couple. He cleared his throat and forced his mind to clear. "A group will go to the helicopter. If we can rig some sort of gurney, we may be able to carry Perry out and all go to the clearing."

She frowned. "With a sniper out there?"

"First thing tomorrow I'll check that station in the tree. I'm guessing I'll find a jerry-rigged weapon and no space for a human shooter." He sure hoped that was the case.

The scenario would at least give them a direction. Someone on foot with a gun could easily pick them off one by one as they lumbered along dragging Perry on a slab.

There was a nightmare thought. A rigged gun had a limited attack range. A human on foot spelled real danger.

"And that means we can walk through the woods."
She rubbed her hands together until the skin turned red.

"I think we need to take the risk." He walked over
and sat next to her. "Speaking of which, you were pretty
impressive today."

"I got lucky."

He slipped his hand over hers and stopped her fidgeting before she rubbed her skin raw. "I'm thinking your
climbing skills and all those years of archery helped."

"I'll give you the archery."

"Not the climbing?"

She shrugged. "I stick with normal climbing now."

"Why?" He knew the story because he'd never stopped
watching over her, making sure she was okay.

Part of the story anyway. He could tell from the nervous energy that she kept part of it trapped inside her and
it needed to come out.

"A burst of sanity?"

His thumb rubbed over the back of her hand, and his
thigh touched hers. "Hope, this is me. I know how much
you love climbing. I've been along with you, seen your
face."

"To be fair, I'm a fan of almost anything that happens outside."

He wasn't buying it, refused to let her dismiss this.
"You excelled at taking groups up. Your dad didn't like
it, but it was a good living."

"Until it wasn't."

The monotone voice tugged at him. "What piece am
I missing?"

"The accident." Her free hand brushed over their
joined ones. "Come on, you talk with my dad, right?
You know about this."

Joel had read the news articles about it and gotten the

basic information from her dad. Joel knew it was a horrible accident—not her fault—but it didn't sound like she did. "I know you took a group up Mt. Rainier and bad weather rolled in."

She sighed and her shoulders fell. "Two men died, Joel."

"You're not responsible for an unexpected snowstorm, Hope."

"But I am the one responsible for knowing when to turn around." She loosened her grip on his hand.

"Wait a minute." He held on, even squeezed her palm until she looked at him again. "I read the file—"

"What are you talking about?"

He refused to be derailed by the rising anger in her voice. "You've tracked me, at least a little, because you know I live in Annapolis. Well, I know what you've been doing since we broke up, and the point is you trained that group and when something happened, a guy panicked and took his friend down the mountain with him."

"We should have—"

"The other people in the group said you insisted everyone go down. You followed your own rules and didn't screw around. The guy ignored you."

"It was as if he expected me to chase him up the mountain."

"Not to speak ill of the dead, but his ego took over. That's on him, not you." Joel had watched her struggle with male stupidity more than once in her work. She had all the skills and knowledge, but you put a bunch of guys together and sometimes a certain type would show off. Add in how pretty she was and some guys underestimated her.

Joel never did. She was stunning and fierce...and he

loved her as much today as he did when he had walked out. Maybe more.

"All he had to do was turn around and slam his ax into the ice." She whispered the words, lost in whatever mental image played in her head. "He was tied to his friend and they both raced down the slope and…"

"Listen to me." Joel's hand went into her hair and he turned her to face him. "I deal with danger and guilt all the time. I know the difference between negligence and horrible tragedy. You lived through the latter."

"It destroyed my love of climbing."

He leaned in and kissed her because he couldn't stand not to right then. "It's too soon to know that."

"I just wanted to start over, find something else I loved, and now this." She tucked her head under his chin.

"Also not your fault."

The vanilla scent of her shampoo and smell of her skin had his mind blanking. He had to close his eyes to stay in comfort mode and away from whatever mode it was that had him wanting to push her back into the sleeping bag.

"The comment is funny coming from you." Her hand pressed against his chest, and her fingers toyed with the neck band of his T-shirt. "You take on the weight of everyone else's sins and let them define your life."

"That's not true." He wouldn't let that be true.

She lifted her head then and stared at him with those big brown eyes. "You left me because of things that have nothing to do with us."

She kissed his chin. Let her fingertips dance over his cheek.

"Hope, don't—"

"You love me." She pressed her fingers to his lips.

He kissed the tips. "Always."

"Yet we're not together."

"My feelings and reality are two different things." The mantra played in his head, but his body and his heart rebelled. The need for her kicked strong enough to knock him over.

Being this close to her, holding her, seemed so easy. Made him doubt everything he believed about how his life should go. How he should stay alone rather than risk dragging someone else into his life.

Bottom line was he could easily become his father one day. The old man had been normal once, or so their old neighbors said. But at some point, he'd lost it. Joel worried every day he'd travel down the same road.

No, he was right. They couldn't make this work. "We're never going to agree on this."

"How about this?" She swept her lips over his, gentle and quick.

His temperature spiked and somewhere in his brain an alarm bell rang. "What are you doing?"

"Wow, it really has been a long time for you, hasn't it?" Her sexy smile promised a sleepless night.

It also smashed through his control with the destructive crush of a bulldozer. "This is a bad idea."

"Then let's do something bad." She slid out of his arms and fell back against the mattress with her hair spilling over the small pillow.

Maybe if he kept saying her name his brain would have time to restart. "Hope…"

Having none of it, she pulled him down on top of her. "You want me. I want you."

He balanced his weight on his elbows and stared down at her. "What we feel is deeper than that, and sleeping together could mess it all up."

It took every last bit of his strength to get the words out. He didn't mean them and hated saying them.

Her arms wrapped around his neck, and her body slid against his. "Do you honestly think our relationship could be a bigger mess than it is?"

"We broke up." But he had nothing left. No way to fight her.

"And neither of us has moved on." She treated him to a lingering kiss. "Do you want me to move on, Joel?"

Hell, no. "You need—"

"You."

The next kiss didn't brush or linger. It burned. Her tongue touched his and her hot mouth had him reeling.

When he lifted his head again he could barely breathe and his brain stuck on permanent misfire. "I have exactly one condom."

Her eyebrow lifted. "I'm a little surprised you have even that."

"Call it wishful thinking, but when I knew I was coming to you—"

"Go get it." She whispered the command against his mouth.

He scrambled out of the bed and grabbed the wallet out of his pocket. After a second, he dropped it on the floor.

Before he could climb back onto the bed, she was there, sitting on the edge. Her fingers went to work on his belt, then his zipper. The screech echoed through the quiet room as she lowered it.

Her hand covered him and her breath blew across his boxer briefs. Looking down and seeing her hair, feeling her soft hand on his erection, proved to be too much. The last of his common sense fled as he threw the condom on the bed and pushed her back.

Hands roamed everywhere. His, hers, it didn't matter. His shirt came off and then hers. It wasn't until he saw her bare skin and the sweet shadow between her breasts that he forced his body to slow down, to savor.

He skimmed his fingers over the smooth skin of the top of her breasts, then slipped a finger inside the edge of a plain white bra. At that moment, the sexiest bra he'd ever seen. With a teasing flick over her nipple through the material, he heard her gasp.

"I can't forget you." His mouth went to her neck as he said the startling truth in a gruff voice.

"Don't."

He felt the tug of his pants and felt them slide down farther on his hips, freeing him. Her hand slipped past the elastic band of his underwear and then she was on him, skin against skin, and he had to grind his back teeth together from ending this too soon.

"I want you." He told her right before he kissed her, not giving him a chance to take it back or her a chance to question.

His lips crossed over hers as the heat rolled through him. A signal went off in his brain. Protection…it was there somewhere. His hand patted the bed, searching for the condom. Adrenaline pounded him and he was about to rip the sleeping bag apart to find it when she picked it up and held it in front of his face.

"Looking for this?"

He didn't say anything. Couldn't. He plucked it out of her hand and tore through the paper. His body was on fire now. He had to have her, to sink into her again.

Desperate to make it good for her, he ran a hand over her stomach and hit the band of her pants. Yeah, those had to come off. He didn't waste a second as he stripped them down, taking her bikini bottoms with them and throwing the rumpled ball to the floor.

Then she was naked and open, her legs falling to

the side to make room for him between them. When he dragged a finger through her heat, her back arched off the bed.

She was wet and ready. She didn't pretend shyness. He could read the need on her face and see the excitement in the pink hue of her skin.

It was all the invitation he needed. Rolling the condom on, he fit his tip to her and pushed. His body plunged into hers as it always had, with a tightness that made a groan rumble up the back of his throat.

The night fell away and the closeness of the other cabins didn't matter. He was back inside her as he'd fantasized about for so long. And he wanted it to last. He stilled, enjoying the feel of her tight body around his.

She pinched his shoulder. "Joel, move."

But his body had already taken over. He pressed in and pulled back out. A steady rhythm gave way to a frantic beating of his blood. Her nails dug into his shoulder as she whispered his name in his ear.

He kissed her, touched her, made love to her as the driving need took over. Tension coiled inside him. The building started in every limb. That's what she did to him. Destroyed his intentions and stole control over his body.

Unable to hold back, he slid a hand between them and touched her. A slight circle with his finger and her head pressed back. When her mouth dropped open he covered it with his, thinking to catch those delicious gasps he loved so much as she found her release.

The orgasm slammed into him a second later. His body let go and his shoulders shook until he thought they wouldn't hold him. With one last push, he surrendered.

His last thought was that he hadn't taken the time to pull his pants off.

Chapter Ten

An alarm buzzed beside her head, breaking into Hope's delicious dream. She thought about throwing it at the wall.

When her eyes opened and she adjusted to the overhead light and darkness outside the window, it all came rushing back. Joel's arm across her stomach. His breath against her neck. The memories of the kissing and touching. Making love with him, feeling him over her. Rolling around after and his cursing once he remembered they only had one condom.

She'd wanted another morning after with him for so long. It was somewhere around three and not yet sunrise, but this was close enough.

Through the waves of anger and hurt all those months ago and every day since, she knew they'd get back to this emotional place. That they weren't over. The real question was how long they could stay in this holding position.

The temptation to hide under the blanket and forget the world and the horrors outside the cabin rushed over her. She hated to wake him, but that was the deal. One person on guard duty, and Cam had been handling that for hours.

Now, deep into the night, rain still pinged against the cabin and the alarm on his simple black watched sounded